Major Marcus Cavanaugh and his company of Buffalo Soldiers entered the walled canyon, and rode down into a windless, ovenlike hotbox filled with boulders. Marcus paused to sweep the rim and walls with field glasses, and saw no signs of life.

The sun was sinking down in the western sky when a sudden shot rang out. Instantly, the troopers' hands were on their carbines' stocks. Eyes searched the cliffs for puffs of smoke.

Then all hell broke loose.

From the cliffs erupted a heavy fusillade, the reports of rifles crackling like strings of firecrackers. Up and down the column several troopers were felled by slugs.

The troopers' Springfields began to boom, and the canyon was filled with acrid smoke. Cavanaugh found it hard to see. There was another roar of concentrated Winchester fire. Slugs beat the surrounding rocks. One officer was punched half around in his saddle, crimson blood blossoming on his dark blue blouse.

Marcus threw up his hand. "Listen to me, men! Renew the charge! Fire and keep firing! Give the savages pure hell!"

The bugle called for the charge.

The Buffalo Soldiers thundered down the canyon, a furious, hurtling avalanche.

Other books in the **ARROW AND SABER** series:

#1:   OUSHATA MASSACRE
#2:   CAVANAUGH'S ISLAND

BATTLE AT
THUNDERHORSE MESA

G.A. CARRINGTON

A DELL BOOK

Special Thanks to Charlie Perlberg

Published by
Dell Publishing
a division of Bantam Doubleday Dell
Publishing Group, Inc.
666 Fifth Avenue
New York, New York 10103

ISBN: 0-440-20381-3

Printed in the United States of America
Published simultaneously in Canada

December 1989

10 9 8 7 6 5 4 3 2 1

KRI

To Marilyn

BATTLE AT
THUNDERHORSE MESA

Chapter One

The white scout, the one the regiment called Dutch Yancy, pointed out a dark speck hanging on the distant rock cliff under the high, hot sky. It was a hundred degrees on the Arizona desert flats at noon, but army clothing made it seem even hotter. Second Lieutenant Clayton LeMay was leading his first patrol against Apache raiders. Sweat steamed under his wide campaign hat like water dribbled onto a griddle, and his skin crawled beneath his dust-caked uniform blouse. It was so hot he could hardly think!

"So what do you make of it?" LeMay called across to Dutch Yancy. Only a yard separated their horses at the head of the halted troop. At the file leaders' backs, twenty cavalrymen slouched in their McClellan saddles and roasted. Theirs was not the task of making decisions. That duty belonged to the young, green officer. LeMay watched the scout's features carefully, the scraggly beard and the leathery, furrowed brow. The pale, glittering eyes swung back his way, but they couldn't be read.

Dutch Yancy shrugged. "Leftenant, you're the feller with the field glasses slung there around your neck. Why not take a peek yourself?"

He said it without humor, and LeMay assumed he wasn't being laughed at. He had to admit that the term "shavetail" could apply to him, and he hoped the quick flush to his face would simply look like additional sunburn. He fumbled out his binoculars and raised them. The distant sandstone ridge leaped close, and the officer's breath hissed in his teeth.

"It's a man!"

"So?"

"Christ, I confess I've never seen the like!" LeMay thrust the glasses at the scout and frowned, fighting back a gorge of bile.

"Nekkid," exclaimed the scout. "Hung upside down. Ain't moving. Injun work, Leftenant. They'll sometimes catch 'em a lone Mex herdsman thisaway."

"What's it, about a mile from here to there? By God, we're going to ride on over. Sergeant!" LeMay called over his shoulder.

The slab-thin man with chevrons on his sleeve urged his mount up along the line. In a few seconds the noncom was at LeMay's side. "Sergeant Seiber, form up columns of four. We're crossing to that ridge."

Seiber's gaze silently met Yancy's, and the officer ceased talking. The scout jumped in. "Leftenant, that ain't a good idea. Them arroyos and outcrops, they make good ambush points. Could be a trap."

"I can't see any hostiles out there."

"Apaches, you don't spot them unless — " the sergeant began.

"Seiber, I don't recall asking your opinion! That man being tortured over there, he might still be alive! The way I see it, the Apaches are long gone. It's a chance I'm willing to take to save a life!"

2

Again the scout and the noncom exchanged glances.

"I said, form up the column, Sergeant, and it's forward ho!"

There was nothing to do but obey. The shavetail was the one who possessed the rank. Seiber grimly wheeled his horse and gave a signal. The column first formed, and then moved out across the barren desert floor. Patched greasewood and ocotillo clumps were the only vegetation as far as their squinting eyes could see. The detachment crawled across the sun-blasted hell.

It took the better part of an hour, so broken was the terrain, but at last Lieutenant LeMay sat his horse at the base of the crumbling outcrop. It amounted to a cliff face, less than a dozen feet tall, but like the backbone of some half-buried ancient monster it stretched — gaunt, yellow — for at least a quarter mile. The troop's approach had been from the west, and now the sun's glare was a brutal punishment.

LeMay pointed his gauntleted hand. "There the poor wretch hangs. We can get to him in a few more minutes."

"I don't like it, sir," grumbled the scout. "There's the arroyo and the — "

"Forward ho-o!" LeMay kicked the big bay's flanks and it moved ahead again. But for jingling bit chains and the creak of saddle leather, the silence was awesome.

As the troop closed distance, their objective came starkly into view. The strung-up victim, dark of skin and scrawny of frame, was of indeterminate age. He hung by one ankle from a taut rawhide thong, arms falling, the free leg bent at a right angle from the stretched torso. The fellow's skin, every inch, was burned and blistered from the sun. The sores would have run pus, but for the body's dehydration.

3

There was a mumbling in the ranks as the cavalry troop moved near. Sergeant Seiber's hand drifted toward his flap holster and encased service revolver.

"I think I heard a groan," the officer said. "Sergeant, have two privates dismount and prepare to climb up."

"I don't like this at all," the scout protested. The leathery face was fixed in a sullen mask.

"I gave an order! It was — "

The rest of the officer's remark was never heard. The ridge above the tightly grouped troop exploded with shrieks and gunfire. From the arroyo to the startled soldiers' left came a deadly fusillade. "Apaches!" bellowed Dutch Yancy, but then an arrow pierced his neck and the scout spilled from his saddle. All up and down the line, bluecoats grabbed frantically for their Springfields.

"Return fire!" shouted Clayton LeMay, his high voice cracking. He held his service revolver tight in his fist. He triggered, blasting air.

Sergeant Seiber wheeled his mount in a circle. "Cover! Take cover! Horse handlers! Down into the gully!" He whipped off three hurried shots with accuracy. A charging redskin yowled and pitched headlong.

The few veteran cavalry kept their cool heads, dismounting in good order and scrambling among some shielding rocks. But the troop had its share of green recruits, and these were stunned. It took the briskly rapped commands of the sergeant to spark the panicked men to action. By then several had dropped, one writhing, two lifeless and still.

"Damn it, get down!" This time Seiber's call was heeded, and the greenies took up sporadic fire. From behind rocks, shrubs, and cutbanks the .45-70 single-shots barked, spewing smoke and flame.

It was enough for every man jack to envy the wielders of repeaters. Still, amid curses and the cries of

4

the wounded, the troopers began to take their toll. Private Tom Cartwright drew a bead on an exposed copper shoulder and jerked his trigger. The Apache's arm was shattered by the heavy slug, and he dropped from view.

Private Nels Olafson fired a round into a yelling, charging Chiricahua's face. The redskin's head exploded in a splash of gore, and the running corpse back-flipped like a shattered doll.

Lieutenant LeMay's complexion had gone suety as he bellied down on the flinty ground. Slugs zipped over the risky dig-in, a deadly hail. "A trap, it was a sneaky trap." The hoarse words rattled in his throat. Out on the flat the dead scout Dutch Yancy sprawled. Other army dead littered the surrounding ground, sprouting arrows like porcupines' quills. The officer's brain reeled. He saw no strategy to be used to get the men out. None.

He had an overwhelming urge to jump up and wave a white flag, but he could still see from his position the suspended Mexican's corpse. It was now apparent that the eyes had been devoured by birds. The herdsman had been thrown over the cliff to die slowly. LeMay wondered if he, taken alive, could bear such torture. But he had to be an example to his men.

"Sergeant Seiber!" LeMay shouted aloud. "We out-number the savages! It's just a raiding party!"

The noncom slipped up the draw and bellied at his side. "True enough — " Seiber's tongue stumbled when called on to utter 'sir.' "But they've gathered in, bunched up on the heights."

"Bunched. That just may be their downfall, Sergeant. If we muster our force, split it in units, we can make a two-pronged charge. Caught in a crossfire, they'll have no choice but cut and run. It'll work! It's got to!"

"Christ, the losses we'll sustain — "

The officer fought to control his fear. "Pass the word. I'll lead the right-wing charge myself!"

"But — "

"Damnit, Seiber, that's an order! Now get going!" He jammed fresh cartridges into his pistol's cylinder.

Five minutes later he called the advance.

As the sergeant had pointed out, there was a steep upslope they had to hike. Baked open ground, it stretched dun-brown in the sun. As the troopers ran, they cast long, surging shadows. There was a peppering volley from above. LeMay ignored all but his sense of duty, mixed as it was with panic. His grit-caked boots skidded, almost spilling him in a patch of soft sand.

An arm's length from the officer, a pair of privates took rounds and fell. One's abdomen erupted great handfuls of intestine. Clayton LeMay brandished his Colt and plunged on. A painted redskin leaped from the crest and bore down at him. A thrown lance darted past his head. LeMay aimed and fired.

The Indian stopped, shrieked, then toppled. A hole in the bare copper chest produced great gouts of blood.

The officer's whole field of vision appeared crimson-tinted. On both sides he saw his men dropping and unhurt soldiers rushing to fill the gaps. The lieutenant and his troops reached the ridge together and swarmed over. The conflict became rough-and-tumble, hand-to-hand. Corporal Joe Hutchins was taken by a war club along his temple. He died mouthing a shrill gurgle. Hans Vanderveen took a slug from a dragoon side arm in an Indian hand. But then LeMay's shot flung the red man back, dead and crumpling. The sharp scent of powder fumes filled the still, hot air.

The savages' line of resistance had given way. The Apaches, outnumbered, fled toward waiting ponies.

"Give chase, men! Give chase!" the lieutenant yelled. Those troopers still upright raised a ragged cheer.

"By God, we did it! Well done, C Company!" Amid drifting smoke, LeMay stood and peered about him. Now that the Indians were gone from the battlefield, there was the appalling aftermath. Wounded soldiers clutched their hurt parts. The scene was repeated on every side.

"Seiber! Is that you?" On the ground near the officer, the sergeant lay outstretched. The noncom's blouse front was no longer blue, but blood-red from at least three wounds. LeMay dropped to one knee, and lifted the man. Seiber's glazed eyes stared at the smooth-cheeked, ash-gray face. The pain-wrung mouth tried for words, but the sergeant twitched, then slumped.

From behind LeMay a raw private queried, "Can we help, sir? It appears the sarge is dead."

"Tell the troop to gather in. Bring up the horses. Fix litters to bear the casualties."

"Yessir!"

Lieutenant LeMay's gaze searched Seiber's pale, slack face, then lifted to the sky. *Goddamn*, he cursed silently, to himself. Then he breathed the word again, this time biting it out. "Goddamn! Goddamn!"

Chapter Two

The major looked up when he heard the shout outside the orderly room. He dropped his pen on the desk and stood. Marcus Anthony Cavanaugh was just a year in his field-grade rank, and retained a healthy curiosity for things that smacked of action. With his tall erect carriage, he crossed swiftly to the door. Opening the desert-dried wood panel, he stepped onto the veranda and peered out across the parade ground of the post.

Under his level kepi's brim, the officer squinted against the eternal Arizona glare. Lightly etched crows' feet were distinct at his eye corners, and a few gray hairs salted his dark-brown thatch. Still, he was quite young for a major, a fact that stung lower officers who'd been many years in rank. Marcus, though, had been in the right place at the right time, seizing opportunity and achieving heroism. Now he found himself posted far from the Cheyennes, the enemy he'd fought so strategically and so well.

They called this land Apacheria. Even at their best, the Apaches were fierce, determined foes. Marcus

8

glanced up at the Stars and Stripes, which hung limp on its staff. The adobe walls did a fine job of blocking the breeze.

A squad of troopers marched vigorously past in dismounted drill, under the scrutiny of a grim-faced corporal. Then the distant shout that Marcus had heard at his desk was repeated, and past the gate-sentries burst a rider on a lathered horse. The animal slid to a haunches-down stop in a billow of sandy dust.

"Dispatch rider," breathed a voice at Marcus's shoulder. Sergeant Major Brody's sun-browned features wore deep creases of concern. "Van Ness of C Company," he muttered. "Lieutenant LeMay and his patrol, then, they've been tastin' trouble?"

"We'll hear in a minute, won't we, sergeant?" Marcus kept his face rigid. The messenger leaped from the saddle and stumbled stiff-legged toward where they stood.

"Where's the colonel, by the way, Brody?" Cavanaugh asked.

"Er, his quarters, I guess."

"So." Marcus had heard the same plenty in the months he'd been the fort's executive officer. The post commander, Lieutenant Colonel Thornhill was all too often indisposed. The messenger panted up the steps and tossed a sloppy salute. Since the man seemed near exhaustion, Marcus let it pass. Unintelligible mouthings burst from the private.

"Van Ness," the sergeant roared. "Settle! Damn it, what's your news?" He turned to a huge clay jug suspended from the rafter, filled its dipper and handed the man a drink. Van Ness splashed his chin and dirt-caked blouse front. The *olla* swayed in its sling.

"C Company — "

"We know your outfit, soldier! Apaches?"

"San Simon Creek. . . . Ambush . . . a dozen or so bucks! Jesus, Sergeant, but it was awful!"

Marcus Cavanaugh listened with close attention.

"Nine troopers killed," the messenger rattled on. "Three wounded. We shot us a few savages, but they scattered and ran. The troop cut up so bad, Lieutenant LeMay, he turned back for the fort."

"Be here in a few hours?"

"By sundown, I reckon."

Marcus gave a curt nod and turned to Brody. "We'll need to see the surgeon's alerted. And Colonel Thornhill, as well."

The sergeant peered around. "Nantaje's band, do you suppose, sir?"

"At least part of it, most likely. We know by now that they're off the reservation." Marcus pinched his lips.

"What about the lieutenant himself?" the sergeant asked the man. "He wounded, too?"

"No, sir. Only mad as hell."

"Go along, then, Private. You're dismissed."

It was going to be a long, hot summer. The Chiricahuas and the outlaws of the Mimbres tribe had begun their raids. Southern Arizona settlers were being harassed and killed, and the red molesters would strike swiftly and then flee. Later, they'd regroup across the border for still more strikes. And the Mexican *Rurales* were buffaloed, too.

Things had gone purely to hell since Chief Cochise had died. Toward the end, the old warrior had led his people onto the white man's reservation. Now the braves wanted their bloody raids again. And Nantaje, the preeminent war leader among them, was eager to lead the slaughter.

The region in the neighborhood of Apache Pass was guarded by Fort Bowie's meager regiment in blue. Enlisted farm lads, immigrants, riffraff — the usual army mix. They'd been shaped up and honed, all right, but the force was still very undermanned. In the short months since he'd been on post, Marcus Cavanaugh had worked wonders. But shorthandedness remained a hard, cold reality.

There was another difficulty the major hadn't originally counted on, but had been confronted with. And he'd be attempting to deal appropriately with it again this afternoon.

"Brody, I'll be dropping by the commander's quarters and giving Colonel Thornhill the bad news."

"Yessir!"

Brody's salute was snappy. The insignia on the sergeant's kepi glittered in the sun. Marcus returned the salute and strode back into headquarters alone. He was hot under the wool, brass-buttoned uniform tunic, but ignored it. In a few minutes he'd cleared his desk of papers. Then he exited again. As he skirted the parade ground he surveyed the vault of sky and the sun's bright disk. His polished Jefferson boots had gained a dusty film.

At last he stood before the commander's house with its trim whitewashed porch and stanchions. The wood had been wagoned in across the desert. A bed of tamarisks maintained by the fatigue details bloomed colorfully against the drab gray of the yard. Marcus mounted three steps to rap gently, twice.

"Come," croaked a low voice beyond the panel.

Marcus Cavanaugh shoved the door inward and entered a drape-dimmed parlor. "Colonel Thornhill?"

The officer on the horsehair settee had loosed his tunic collar, and the jacket was far from crisp. He struggled hurriedly to straighten slack and hunched shoulders, but any military bearing was gone. The face was of a man in his fifties, deeply tanned from nearly three decades spent on frontier posts. The eyes seemed somehow older than the rest of Franklin Thornhill. He didn't rise to greet his visitor. The whiskey bottle resting beside him was drained.

"Yes, Major, has something gone wrong? You've never troubled me at my quarters before. In fact, have you even been in this house since my Becky died?"

"Not in the last three months, no sir."

The senior officer rammed his fist in his palm. "Goddamn the sickness that carried her off! Surgeon Cuppenwaldo couldn't do a thing!"

Marcus Cavanaugh waited patiently. "I know I should do better," Thornhill muttered. "But without my wife, something's somehow died in me. Ought to quit my command."

Marcus spoke up briskly. "A half year before a scheduled retirement, Colonel? Lose your pension from the War Department? You've been a fine officer far too long to throw all that away."

"So you're determined to help an old soldier in his hour of need? Well, we'll see. Major, why did you come today?"

Cavanaugh relayed Lieutenant LeMay's message, adding: "It could shape up to a rough summer with this Chiricahua Apache business, sir. Bowie is damned shorthanded, with no replacements for desertions for a good long while. And Nantaje's grown so bold as to jump a troop out on the scout."

"Don't worry on my condition at the moment, mister. I'll be at my desk to take LeMay's report when he rides in."

"Yes, sir. Thank you, sir."

The colonel threw Marcus a casual salute.

On the veranda the young major paused to adjust his hat and listen. From inside the commander's parlor came a thud and a groan. Marcus shook his head and went down the steps, saluting a passing corporal bound for the quartermaster's storehouse. He had plenty to do before the sun set below the sawtooth range. Even if it was no more than routine pencil-pushing.

When he reached the rambling structure that housed the headquarters office, a group of junior officers had gathered in the shade of the brown adobe wall. From the buzz of conversation as he passed, Marcus overheard their concerns. Indians, the projected summer campaign, the severe shortage of men. They knew of the dispatch rider's arrival, as was natural. Such news always spread like wildfire through frontier posts.

Marcus saw no sense in spending time with the talkers. He mounted the steps with eyes fixed straight ahead and proceeded inside. The duty officer's desk, next to his own, was now occupied. A chunky man whose shoulders carried twin gold bars glanced up and scowled. The gray-peppered sideburns bristled.

"Major."

"Afternoon, Captain," Marcus greeted the older man.

Captain Shelby Frye, fairly fresh from Eastern duty — Washington, D. C. — was an embittered man. Brevetted a full colonel for his heroism at Antietam, his rank had reverted at return of peace. Desk-bound duties in the capitol had proved barren. He'd won no more promotions. Marcus understood that the man had requested frontier posting as a last desperate ploy.

If the battlefield was a stage for advancement, the man was determined to have his one last chance. The unique thing about this decision, however, was his immature and fragile wife. That Sophia Frye should be put to such discomforts — but that was the couple's problem. Marcus was not going to involve himself.

"I want to be here when LeMay reports to the old man," Frye said abruptly. Marcus peered over his shoulder as he hung up his kepi.

"I've no objection."

13

"That's good." The fleshy pink face, as yet not burned brown, assumed a smile. "Looks like action's on its way, hey, Major?"

Marcus Cavanaugh sat down. "Doubtless."

"You were posted here way back last fall. Have had the opportunity by now to study the usual moves of the hostiles. Why haven't we been able beat them?"

"Not lack of bravery, mister. And Colonel Thornhill's a hell of a fine field tactician. Nantaje's a wily adversary, that's for sure. And the red man's fighting on his own home ground. Attack and fly, that's his method. Avoid the large decisive battles. And so far, it's worked."

"Word in Washington before I came out was — "

Marcus' interest rose. "Yes? Go on."

"Well you can guess how talk in Indian Affairs, even Congress, might run. Results wanted from the money spent. That sort of thing. But I'll assure you of this, Major Cavanaugh, pressure's rising to see the savages exterminated, wiped out. The reservation system's seen as an inadequate solution. Look what's happened here in A.T."

"Arizona Territory has its share of woes, among them undermanned garrisons."

"If predictions hold, and a bureaucrat's sent out — " The jaded company-grade officer broke off. Marcus was intrigued by Frye's words, but a din in the compound pulled both men to their feet. Hoofbeats.

Through the window could be seen the gate, and a column of exhausted, dust-grimed men and mounts marching through it. C Company, Cavalry, Bowie, Arizona Territory, had returned from patrol. Second Lieutenant Clayton LeMay, West Point, '74, swung down wearily from his saddle. Marcus saw a badly bloodstained uniform front under a strained, pale face.

He crossed the floor in long-legged, swift strides, and plunged outside. He plowed past the crowd of blue-

14

coated men. The young officer speared him with a hostile stare.

"Are you — ?"

"Alive and unhurt, Major. This blood's my sergeant's. Poor wretch died in my arms." Lieutenant LeMay marched past woodenly, and went into the headquarters building.

Recalling the bright youngster riding out at the head of his patrol, Marcus shook his head. Never had he seen a man's face age so in just three days.

"Well now, Lieutenant. Let's have your report."

Colonel Thornhill sat behind his desk, rigid, hollow-eyed in a freshly brushed uniform. The silver oak leaves on his shoulder boards winked in the soft lamplight. Dusk had come. Along one shadowed wall Marcus and Frye stood, their faces grim. In the center of the room LeMay broke his stiff salute, but remained at attention. There had been no opportunity to change clothes. About him clung the rank odors of horses, sweat, and blood.

"Well, mister. Proceed."

"Colonel, I'll get directly to the skirmish." LeMay spoke slowly, as if in a trance. "Tuesday, yesterday — that's when it happened. Ten men killed, three took wounds as the troop fought off an ambush. Included in the dead were Sergeant Sieber and Dutch Yancy."

"The scout?"

"The scout. He took an arrow early. We were under this tall rock cliff, broken ground, arroyos — "

The commanding officer interrupted. "Yancy was always been a canny man. How did it happen, I wonder, your finding yourselves in a place for ambush?"

LeMay hesitated slightly. He knew the men would be spreading the truth about the engagement anyway. There was no use trying to deceive his superiors. "Well,

15

sir, I — we — spotted a civilian the Indians had strung up to let die. We — I — decided to go have a close-up look. As we approached, the terrain grew rough and — "

"You're new on the frontier, Lieutenant. What did your sergeant have to say?"

"He was reluctant to proceed, sir. He and the scout both. I put them in their place."

"And led them into an Apache trap?"

"We might've been able to save a life."

Colonel Thornhill scowled. "The civilian, he was alive, then?"

"As it turned out, no, he wasn't, sir."

"So the result you achieved was the death of ten troopers." Thornhill drummed his fingers on the desktop. "Oh, and three wounded. Surgeon says one will have to lose an arm. Your exploit looks like foolishness to me, mister, foolishness! Close to half a company wiped out!"

"The troop wasn't up to staff, sir."

"All the more reason not to throw lives away!" Then, more calmly, Thornhill said, "Well, what's done is done. That's all for now, LeMay. Paperwork tomorrow. Maybe paperwork for a good long while to come." Thornhill glanced at the captain and major. Both stood there, watching, impassive as the mud-brick wall.

Not so the shavetail. "Sir! I tried to do my best!"

"They teach excuse-making these days at West Point?"

"Permission to be dismissed?"

"Granted." Thornhill returned the lieutenant's salute. The young man turned on his heel and marched out. When the door had closed, the colonel looked at the other two officers. "Inexperience. The youngster's going through a damned bad time."

"But he'll learn."

"He'll have to learn, by God!"

Captain Shelby Frye stepped forward. "Colonel, I'm willing to lead a company out on the scouts. I request again to be permitted to do so. Sir?"

"Captain, I'll consider it. Be letting you know in a few days. As for right now, it's nearly supper hour. You have a wife on the post, man. Don't keep her waiting."

A crisp "Yes, sir!" That left the commander and his second in command together.

"He's a desk man, is Captain Frye. I can read his kind like a book. Another fool, out from Washington to bid for glory. But I just may end by putting him on a horse if this border region blows up."

"Jumping and whipping LeMay's patrol as he did," Marcus observed, "Nantaje has to have grown pretty bold."

The colonel's look saddened. "Marcus, the summer ahead? It's bound to be sheer hell."

Clayton LeMay stumbled through the darkness between the barracks and the bachelor officer's quarters. Night shrouded the post under the vault of star-flecked sky. Splashes of light through the windows left bright rectangles on the ground, but the shavetail avoided them. He also avoided the voices of officers and enlisted men as they hurried on their way to mess.

LeMay told himself that he didn't need their arrogant, righteous looks. And he wasn't going to let anyone stop him from what he meant to do. It was far too late for that.

The heavy weapon in his flap holster slapped his thigh as he turned in between looming buildings. The quartermaster's stores and the stables. When he moved into the blackest shadows he was already palming the .45 issue Colt. He hadn't cleaned his side arm since the

Indian fray, but merely reloaded hastily. That would suffice.

What he'd been through was disgrace. He'd glimpsed the eyes of that blank-faced major as he'd given his report. Cavanaugh, that cool son of a bitch! The famous winner of the medal for heroism. A gold-leaf major at the age of thirty. A brilliant career.

He heard a laugh off somewhere in the distance. Closer by in the compound paddock, a gelding stamped and blew. Lieutenant LeMay brought the gun up from his side, popped the muzzle into his mouth and drew a deep, wheezing breath.

Clayton LeMay stroked the trigger of his Colt, a feather-gentle gesture. Hammered sharply, the shell went off with a crash. The lieutenant's brain winked out just as his skull exploded.

Following the sound of the gunshot, Major Marcus Cavanaugh was first to reach the corpse.

Chapter Three

The party from Washington arrived at Fort Bowie in the middle of the month. Warned by an advance messenger, Thornhill and Marcus had doubled up on inspections and seen to it that the men were drilled till they were sore. All the horses at Fort Bowie were curried till their hides shone. The post was in order from front to back and top to bottom. Still, it was the Arizona desert in early summer. The blazing heat slammed down mightily, and the air rained dust.

The commanding officer ordered out the regimental band when the visitors were sighted out across the flat. The Dougherty sprung ambulance with its Interior Department human cargo rolled into the compound to the stirring musical notes of "The Gal I Left Behind Me."

As the canvas-curtained wagon lurched to a stop, the trooper escort filed off to one side. An officer snapped out an order, and the soldiers lined up on fagged and sweating horses. Guidons waved. There was an elaborate exchange of salutes. From the veranda of the compact headquarters structure, two men descended. The officers' uniforms were spit-and-polish perfect, and their insignia glittered.

"Hiram Titus. Ever hear of him?" Colonel Thornhill muttered to Marcus as they stalked across the parade.

"I know as much as you," the young major responded quietly. "Department of the Interior. Fact-gathering travels. Big man in the capital."

"He'd have the President's ear, then?"

"That's most likely, Colonel."

The plump, balding man in the brown serge suit negotiated the long step from the wagon bed to the ground. And then, from inside the Dougherty, a younger, more flashy civilian emerged. Unlike the bulky bureaucrat, this one moved with fluid ease. They were of a kind, though. Physically soft, perhaps, but mentally tough. Stubborn, even. Steeped in Eastern ways, pitifully ignorant of the West. It wasn't a good combination for handling Indians, whether in war or peace.

The commander and the executive officer took the newcomers' handshakes and introductions. "I'm Hiram Titus, at your service, Colonel and Major. And my companion on this trip is Mr. Moody Pearson, here. I'm Interior, of course. Mr. Pearson isn't government. He represents railroad interests."

"Pleased to meet you both. Pleased, indeed." Frank Thornhill wore a broad, but false, smile. "Lieutenant Colonel Thornhill. My executive officer at Fort Bowie is Major Cavanaugh, here. I suggest we adjourn to my office, gentlemen. The heat will be no worse indoors."

"Delighted."

Five minutes later, the civilians were seated in straight chairs before the commander's desk. An orderly passed a tray of cool tea. Captain Frye had joined the group and stood by with Marcus, militarily square-shouldered but at ease. The topic was the harshly hot Arizona climate and discomforts of the region in gen-

20

eral. Such were completely unknown in the large cities back East, the officers were bluntly told. Then the colonel cleared his throat and abruptly changed the subject.

"The dispatches that preceded your arrival, gentlemen. They let us know we should expect you, but declined to spell out exactly why. You're not War Department, but as you say, Department of the Interior. My guess is, in this case that means the Bureau of Indian Affairs. Do you wish to provide us more details?"

"Not a bad idea, Colonel Thornhill," Hiram Titus said. He ran smooth hands along smooth cheeks and scratched his gleaming crown. From the way he squirmed when he talked, Marcus suspected the bureaucrat's waistcoat was too tight. But then, neither did the thinner and more fit one appear overly comfortable.

Titus began to speak in a loud politician's voice. "Washington is most concerned over the Indian problem in the Arizona District, colonel. That the reservations, from the large one at San Carlos to the several smaller ones, aren't containing the more unruly and bloodthirsty of the Apaches. And neither does the Army seem able to run down the raiders who are attacking the whites. To come to the point, alternative courses of action are now being weighed in the capitol. A first-hand inspection of the situation out here — that's the reason for my tour."

Thornhill glanced at Marcus, then back at Titus. "What kind of alternatives, may I ask?"

A smile that was like a grimace. "They range from a stricter confinement of the Apache peoples on the reservations that already exist here, to a massive transplantation of them to another part of the country — the Indian Nation, perhaps. At present I happen to support what seems a very practical middle-road expedient, a closer grouping-together of the various bands at just one large agency like the San Carlos. Then all the redskins will be easy to keep tabs on with soldiers and native police."

Marcus and the colonel exchanged glances. "It's believed, then, Mr. Titus," Thornhill objected, "that the San Carlos tract can support so large a group? Almost the entire forty thousand acres is barren wasteland: bitter cold in winter, and in the summer a virtual broiling hell. The game to be hunted is almost gone, and the patchy corn crops invariably fail. Plus, the Apache people consists of many tribes — the Mimbres and the Chiricahua and Ariraipa, the Walapai, Coyotero, and White Mountain bands, to name a few. They've never gotten along well with each other."

The hefty bureaucrat shrugged. "The policy would free other areas of the territory for settlement by whites. Railroads would be built. There'll be an era of tremendous prosperity."

With the mention of railroads, Thornhill's chin bobbed. Moody Pearson simply sat straight and appeared smug. Over beside Marcus, Captain Frye was hanging on every word. "Ah, yes, railroads," the post commander snapped. "The realm of our other visitor, isn't it? I suppose, Mr. Pearson, that on these present travels you're seeking suitable rights-of-way?"

Pearson had a thin, reedy voice. "Of course, Colonel, I'm making use of opportunities that fall my way. I talk to leading townspeople and landowners wherever I go."

"Naturally. But both you men must be aware that the present reservations are defined by treaties with the tribes."

Hiram Titus raised a finger. "Remember one thing. Who were the treaties with Indians signed by? Chieftains who're savages, no more, no less. Isn't it true — and I ask every military man present — that the chiefs are the tribes' bona fide leaders? I mean, accepted as such!"

Frye's face pinched in thought, but Marcus spoke up. "Mr. Titus, I see what you're driving at. Bands of Indians out here aren't well organized, it's true. Not in the way civilized nations are. They have their war chiefs to lead raids, but even then it's up to each buck whether or not he'll fall in with some plan. Just the same, once the treaty makers agree to terms, those terms should be binding for our government, too."

"If you aim to criticize the Indian policy of these United States, Major Cavanaugh — "

"I'm not going that far, sir. Just stating a bit of logic."

"Personal logic, perhaps. I wouldn't want to think the savages have an advocate on this post."

"You're mistaken, Mr. Titus," the colonel put in, "if you think Marcus Cavanaugh is soft on Apaches. Fact is, he's as hard an Indian fighter as they come, as his record certainly shows! But what he's driving at now makes sense. He isn't being pitying, he's being practical. Hungry and betrayed Apaches are hard-to-control Apaches.

"It's simply unwise to force the different tribes to live in close proximity. If shared misery should cause the rivals to mass in alliance, they could send the entire border country up in flames. Once they're all off the reservation, they'd be operating out of badlands and mountain strongholds. Most hard to send troops against successfully. Then even a regiment at full strength would be hard-pressed to root them out."

"And you're having sufficient troubles now, I hear? I've read even in the Eastern newspapers of your arch-foe Nantaje's depredations."

"As we all well know on this post!" Thornhill affirmed. "A cavalry troop was attacked last week, and

23

yes, there were casualties. The men lost aren't likely to be replaced."

"Nantaje's one bitter Chiricahua," Marcus said.

By now both civilians' restlessness was showing. Pearson appeared especially dour. Hiram Titus finally moved to close the meeting. "Ah, yes. As usual, a host of problems. Well, as I say, I'm in this territory to examine all the facts." The thick lips of the Bureau man compressed. "Colonel, Mr. Pearson and I have had a tiring journey. I wonder if we might adjourn? A bath where we'll be rooming and some rest, and then this evening's feast. I'm quite looking forward to the occasion"

"Yes, of course, gentlemen," Thornhill said. "Captain Frye will show you to the quarters that have been assigned."

At the others' departure, Thornhill and Marcus were alone in the hot, sparse room.

"Well!" The colonel pulled a bottle from a desk drawer and filled a glass. "What do you think, Major?"

"About this evening's 'feast' at Fort Bowie's officers' mess?" Marcus grinned. "I think guests who are finicky may be disappointed."

"To the President," was the toast that Hiram Titus proposed, and the massed officers in the antler-bedecked dining room stood and raised their glasses. The long central table was covered by a snowy linen cloth, the Army's best quality. The light from three overhead lamps was reflected in tall flower vases.

Most of the plates had been emptied, as had the large serving platters stacked now on the sideboards. Remains of uneaten antelope haunch had been gathered up by the waiters and lay ready to be carried off, and eaten by the kitchen staff, or saved. The assembled officers of Fort Bowie possessed stomachs stuffed with game and fresh bread and vegetables. They'd managed to devour

24

in the course of an hour the post gardeners' crop for the week. They were satisfied.

That the non-officers of the garrison had dined — always dined — on plain salt pork and beans, troubled few at this banquet spread for dignitaries. Yet, did the dignitaries appreciate the fare? Marcus Cavanaugh had to wonder as he drank off his brandy in honor of Ulysses S. Grant. The expression on the fat face of Hiram Titus matched the gaunt one of Moody Pearson. And neither the government bureaucrat nor the railroad man appeared more or less than sour.

But now Colonel Thornhill had taken the floor and was quietly speechifying. His subject was the honor endowed to Fort Bowie this day and the days ahead. The visitors would be made acquainted with the military tasks relating to the Apache problem. They'd see firsthand the spine-cracking discipline that made the regiment work. And see, as well, how a first-class fighting force made do with short numbers in the conflict against the formidable foe, Nantaje.

To the next proposed leg of their mission — the San Carlos Reservation — the Bowie commander gave short mention. Hopefully Hiram and Pearson would learn enough of the place when they traveled there.

Marcus was surprised to see Titus nudge his thin companion. Pearson hauled to his feet and mustered a wide smile as he began to talk. He thanked the officers of the Sixth for their hospitality, then turned to his particular specialty, railroads. "The best interests of the entire nation lie in a complete system," he said nasally. "Once the lands held siege by Apache rampagers in Arizona Territory are made safe, there'll dawn a new age for peaceful settlement, and the railroads will be there." He stressed the country's need for a transcontinental southern route, then closed, "And it all depends, yes, on you fighting men, this great good that is in store for our country! May the redskin go down to total defeat."

There was polite applause.

The cigars and the whiskey came out, and the conviviality increased. Colonel Thornhill showed remarkable restraint, Marcus thought. He was paying more attention to Titus's small talk than to becoming seriously liquored up. If Cavanaugh knew his superior, though, later — in private — the colonel would drink himself to sleep. But the most surprising thing to the young major was Shelby Frye and Moody Pearson getting their heads together. The pair apparently had much more in common than their bushy, flowing sideburns.

As the hours passed, the conversation dulled, but showed no signs of abating. The hall smelled of strong tobacco and liquor fumes. Marcus slipped out into the black, clear night. From the edge of the parade he peered across to the outer adobe wall and saw the silhouettes of sentries against the blazing stars. The air had cooled off pleasantly.

"Major Cavanaugh, is that you?" The voice from the shadows was melodious and feminine. Marcus recognized it.

"Mrs. Frye? You out walking, too?"

She moved from darkness beside the house wall to the clearer walkway. "Yes, I felt like some fresh air. I thought my husband would be home by now."

"Well, the talk's been stimulating over at the reception. Our visitors on the post are distinguished men from Washington. The captain may have known one from the years that he was stationed there himself."

She'd drawn so close that Marcus glimpsed her smile despite the darkness. She was a pretty, petite woman, Sophia Frye, and he was forced to look down at her. He caught her lavender scent just as she laughed.

"Perhaps. When we lived in the capital, Shelby's acquaintances were always wider than mine. My own friends were all associated with the Army, wives and their officer husbands. Shelby strove to cultivate the lawmakers."

"Political connections. It's one way for a man to get ahead."

"For Shelby it never seemed to quite work."

Marcus turned to go. "Well, I ought to be getting back to the others — "

"Oh, please wait, won't you?"

"There's something wrong?"

"Only — I'm lonely. Since we came out here, Shelby's been so remote. So wrapped up in his career. I'm afraid I feel rather excluded. Major Marcus, sometimes . . . sometimes — "

Now he was very certain that it was time to go. "Mrs. Frye, I'll speak to your husband," he told her. "Drop some hints. But I prefer not to let him know that we've had this talk. Post discipline is very important. And I'm sure your spirits will be picking up directly, ma'am."

"It's true, the colonel asked us to do the entertaining tomorrow," Sophia Frye said. "Shelby and I, we'll be host and hostess of a small dinner for Mr. Titus and Mr. Pearson. Colonel Thornhill's wife being dead, I'm the next-ranking officer's wife here at Bowie, you know." He caught a stammer in her words. "I mean, you're the executive officer, Marcus, it's true, but you're not married. Well, I am looking forward to tomorrow's soiree."

"I'm sure you are."

Jesus, he thought as he strode away. *Trouble on the horizon.* Marcus liked women well enough, but he was far too clear-headed to take chances with his career.

As he neared the officer's mess he found himself disinclined to join the group inside. The trumpeter would be blowing the call to quarters soon anyway, and

27

there was something to be said for being well rested in the morning and unclouded of brain. Marcus turned his steps toward his own quarters, and met a reeling corporal fresh from the sutler's saloon.

A ragged salute was given. Marcus returned it. "Careful, there, my lad."

"Y-yessir!"

The silvery notes of the call to quarters started to ring on the clear air now.

Suddenly Marcus Cavanaugh felt very tired indeed.

Chapter Four

Reveille jarred Marcus — and the whole fort with him — from the jaws of sleep before the sun had even risen above the eastern hills. The executive officer of Bowie pushed his head from his pillow and surveyed his Spartan room in the bachelor officers' quarters with lidded eyes. He'd been rising at ungodly hours since his first days at West Point and, thank God, was finally getting used to it. He had to admit there was something bracing about the air in Arizona, at least in the cool, fresh, early-morning hours.

Of course, when the shimmering heat was pounding down later in the day, then he'd be able to find little to praise in the desert climate.

He rolled from the hard bed to stand at the washstand with its chipped water pan and ewer. He spent the next ten minutes carefully wielding his ivory-handled razor in its appointed task. He donned his uniform and before exiting jammed on the kepi that comprised his headgear when he was inside the walls of the post. After a latrine stop, he made his way to breakfast mess.

His stomach satisfied, Marcus skirted the quadrangle just as the junior-officer noncoms were shaping up some companies for a morning routine of dismounted drill. It was one of the things he loved about army life, the hustle-bustle, the sharply barked commands that snapped men into strict, straight formations and sent them marching. But unlike many officers, Major Cavanaugh wasn't in love with drill for drill's sake, any more than he'd advocate monotonous, harsh punishment as an "uplifting" way of life.

No, this, like every form of spit-and-polish discipline, he viewed as means to an end. Discipline was the single most essential element of an effective fighting machine.

Marcus Cavanaugh was proud of what he was watching. The cavalrymen of Fort Bowie were doing themselves proud, as they doubtless would again in full-dress uniforms later on in the day. The visit of the high Indian Affairs official provided a worthy occasion for a formal inspection and dress review, so the commander had duly ordered one. American flags and company guidons would wave bravely, and the band would play. And doubtless, too, a good many privates would spend the whole grand-appearing exercise cursing under their breath. In spite of the benefits, some of them resented working for their thirteen dollars' monthly soldier's pay.

Marcus energetically took the headquarters steps two at a time, threw the orderly a salute, and passed directly into the presence of Colonel Thornhill.

"Good morning, Major," the commander said, looking up from the sheaf of papers that he held.

"Good morning, sir." Both the officers' salutes were equal in briskness, and their smiles of good humor equally sincere. All things considered, the two had a good working relationship. "Our civilian friends not turned out yet?" Marcus asked wonderingly. "I thought an early meeting was on the schedule. A lot needs to be accomplished today, as I recall."

"Before Titus, Pearson, and company head on their way to Camp Grant, the San Carlos Reservation, and points north?" The older man shrugged. "So they were saying so emphatically last night. And yet they choose to sleep late. I have Sergeant Plover waiting at their quarters doors to hustle them along as best he may."

Marcus drew up a chair to face his superior across the desk. "At least we can exchange private views after sleeping on what happened yesterday. Colonel, what's the reason the railroad fellow's keeping company with Titus on this trip? The government man's fact-finding would seem able to do without him. He just tags along and keeps his mouth shut."

"Oh, I suspect Pearson accomplishes most when those two are between forts and calling on the more important towns. If I know his type, he keeps busy greasing political axles with smooth promises. Even making sly option deals for privately owned property. The fact remains, Marcus, any tracks to be laid across this territory will need to go through Indian-occupied land, and that means the reservations. And yet, peace in the territory depends on the Apaches' good behavior." The colonel's brow folded in a frown. "And, of course, they behave best when the white man honors his treaties, keeps out of their rancherias, and off their hunting grounds."

"Looks like a dilemma."

"And a damned hard one to crack." A glance cast through the window caused Thornhill to edge his chair back and climb stiffly to his feet. "I see the dignitaries coming along the quad."

With the shuffling of city shoes and a few words on the veranda, the Easterners were ushered in. Hiram Titus's mood was less than pleasant, and the greetings

31

were perfunctory. When handshakes were exchanged, Moody Pearson laid down some rolled-up maps he carried.

"If you'll take your chairs, gentlemen?" invited the colonel. "I believe we have a full agenda if we're to be finished for this afternoon's regimental review."

"Whatever happens," Hiram Titus said, "I mean to be in my wagon and rolling out first thing tomorrow morning. I've conveyed that to the leader of my escort so that he'll have the men ready sharp and prompt. My schedule here in the West doesn't allow much leeway. I plan to be in San Francisco on the fifteenth."

"For the purpose — ?"

"You may well wear that concerned look on your face, Colonel. You anticipate what I have to say. I'm to meet in the California capital with General Grummond, commander of the Army's Division of the Pacific. I'll make a report and confer with the general, and afterward we'll both be in telegraph contact with Washington. The government has had enough of Indian problems."

"Everything's being done that a short-manned regiment can do!"

"I'm sure you're doing all that you feel able to, Colonel."

For an unexplained reason, Mr. Moody Pearson smiled.

"If you have ideas, Mr. Titus," Thornhill snapped, "of somehow using your authority in the bureau that controls the reservations — "

"I'll go so far as to say this! Changes are needed!"

Colonel Thornhill retorted hotly. "Apache warriors number many, many hundreds in these parts, mister, and they excel in hit-and-run fighting. They know this country like they know the backs of their hands, and what's more, they know how to live off it, as white army men never can. Right now most happen to be living peaceably on reservations. I hate to think of the hell that would break out, trying to crowd them all onto the wasteland called San Carlos."

"I believe the tribes' terms permit them no warlike acts. Aren't the acts of this Nantaje warlike? How many herdsmen and miners and yes, soldiers, need to die before you realize, Colonel, that the only good Indian is a dead Indian, and that no savage can be trusted as far as you can throw one of their miserable lodges?"

Marcus Cavanaugh found it impossible not to interrupt. "If I may be permitted, sir?" His face took on a hard, cold edge. "The fact is, Mr. Titus, that the Army employs a number of Apache scouts now, and finds them entirely reliable. Men mostly of the Mescalero and White Mountain bands. They've been sent on missions in groups and singly to nab tribal lawbreakers, and have proved willing even to fetch their own brothers back in chains. And we're working together to corral the rampaging broncos. If the government wants to help the situation, we could use more troops."

Hiram Titus pushed his fat face in a frown. "An expensive thing to do, provide more soldiers. They're spread thinly at every fort or outpost between the Mexican and Canadian borders. There could be a better way than just sending down more men, Major." At that he turned to Marcus's commander. "But first let's get down to business of a different kind. Colonel, Mr. Pearson has brought a few maps with him. He'll lay out for you possible routes for a transcontinental line. I'll want your comments."

"I trust no favored right-of-way crosses reservation lands."

"Oh, but indeed some do. That's where your advice comes in. I welcome hearing military strategies that might be used against the tribes."

33

It turned out to be a long, frustrating morning for the colonel and the major, and late in the session Captain Frye was called in as well. Frye's position as adjutant kept him current with situations of supply, both at Bowie, other Arizona army posts, and to some extent at the Warm Springs and San Carlos agencies. At last the large Regulator clock on the wall read noon.

"I presume we can lay aside our differences, gentlemen," Thornhill said, "while we partake of lunch."

"Declare a truce?" The Indian Affairs man dropped his sour expression. "Since the business at hand is about concluded, the idea's a good one."

"Concluded?" asked the colonel. "I don't believe we've resolved all our differences."

"Ah, but Colonel Thornhill — and Major Cavanaugh — that isn't the point. What I came to Fort Bowie for, the information gathering, I feel I've about done. What remains is to behold the troops in review, see the caliber of soldier you're putting into the field. Dinner tonight, I understand, will be at Captain Frye's, you in attendance, together with certain married officers and their wives. I'm looking forward to hearing the females' frothy chatter."

Thornhill clenched his teeth, but managed a smile.

As the group made their way to the officers' mess, heat and glare slammed from the sky as if it were the open door of a furnace.

The parade ground, flat and dusty, baked under the high, hot afternoon sun. It was time for the full-dress review for the garrison of Fort Bowie. The light glinting on epaulets, weapons, and shiny accoutrements winked and stabbed the eyes. On high, the flags waved. The gleaming horns and drums of the regimental band filled the heavy air with martial music. All twelve companies of the regiment were drawn up in a rigidly lined forma-

34

tion. They numbered less than official strength, but were imposing nonetheless. More than eight hundred men were togged out in blue Army dress uniforms trimmed with bright cavalry yellow. Their tall hard helmets were topped by yellow-dyed horsehair plumes. The men would have been an imposing sight even on the Washington Post mall.

The music to "The Gal I Left Behind Me" concluded with a final blare. The men stayed at attention before the color guard, the men who carried American flag and the blue regimental flag with its large embroidered eagle. A trumpeter paced two steps forward from the band's rank, put his brass bugle to his lips, and blew the prescribed call. Major Marcus Cavanaugh marched forward briskly, sheathed saber brushing his striding thigh. He delivered his salute to the commanding colonel and took Thornhill's energetic, crisp return. As the sergeants readied their troops to march, the top officers joined the Fort's civilian guests.

"An impressive display, Colonel," acknowledged Hiram Titus. Standing beside the bureaucrat's round, plump shoulder, Moody Pearson agreed. "I have but one remark, and it's on the presence of the rabble." His thrusting chin pointed across the compound toward a copper-skinned group with long manes the color of ravens' wings.

The indicated men didn't wear blue woolens, dress or otherwise. The only Army-issue things about them were the pistols and rifles they carried, and the cartridge belts cinched tightly around their waists. The remainder of the costumes consisted of bright shirts, breechclouts, calf-high moccasins — ragtag Apache garb. The notion of uniform was seen in only one item of apparel. Each man's brow was crossed by a twisted headband of red calico.

"Our force of Apache scouts? I'd not call them rabble, Mr. Titus. They're Major Cavanaugh's pride and joy. His and Lieutenant Aaron Neel's."

"Neel has worked wonders with them in the field," Marcus put in. "And they're absolutely devoted to their commander, giving him as much respect as he gives them."

"Indeed?" Titus's lips pinched and his nose lifted. "They don't live inside the confines of the fort, I hope?"

"Outside the walls. Traditional wickiup dwellings are their own preference."

"At least the whites can rest somewhat easily."

Marcus Cavanaugh bristled. "By act of Congress those Indian scouts are Army members, Mr. Titus. They earn and draw pay as regular soldiers."

"Indeed? The same law, I wonder, that created six regiments of former Negro slaves?"

"I don't believe it's the same law, no, sir."

"Black men and red men now fighting for the government." Hiram Titus shook his head glumly. "Fool lawmakers. Fools." Out on the field, Sergeant Major Brody bawled. Rifles were slapped and shouldered, and the troopers answered the command and wheeled about. The flank formations broke and marched. Lieutenants Claypoole and Durkey led their companies past with pride. Behind them, more double columns continued to fall in step.

"Ah, the parade," Hiram Titus said with a sigh. The civilians smiled at one another and dabbed perspiring brows. "As a lad I always loved parades. I'll never forget President Grant's most imposing inaugural."

Marcus and Thornhill drew to attention, stiffly erect, eyes fixed straight ahead.

The sun was sinking rapidly and the sky was a fiery gold. Marcus Cavanaugh and Colonel Frank Thornhill walked with an easy pace down the path toward head-quarters. The civilians had preceded them, insisting on a need to change into fresh stiff-collared shirts before joining the ladies. Marcus would have appreciated more comfort, not less.

The scratchy wool of the sweatbox called a dress tunic chafed at the major's wrists and neck. Dampness squished inside his boots. The plumed helmet weighed on the head like a crown of lead. He meant to change quickly in his quarters to a single-breasted coat without the heavy braid and epaulets. And of course, he would abandon his saber, which was only for show.

As usual, the commander registered no sign of heat distress. Marcus read in his eyes, though, that he was craving a tot of good strong drink.

"You go along to quarters, Major," Thornhill said. "I must stop a few minutes by my office. I'll be seeing you at the Fryes' house directly. Mistress Sophia's roast of beef should be a treat fit for a king."

Marcus was about to agree on the adjutant's wife's cooking skills when he saw the orderly coming at a run. The corporal hove up with his hand raised in salute, and waited respectfully.

"Yes, Fane, what is it?" Thornhill was by now accustomed to the noncom's formal manner.

"The sutler, he's sent a message over," the man burst out. "Says he's got him standing orders that whenever a certain man comes into his saloon for a drink — "

"Lord," Marcus Cavanaugh declared. "It's happened? Harry Gougan's on the post?"

"None other than the 'man mountain,'" the corporal affirmed. "The sutler claims he's already emptied a jug, and that the forty-rod whiskey ain't bound to last too long."

The colonel bobbed his helmet. "You'd better get right over there, Major. You're the Army's prime contact with this fellow. Somehow, you manage to get along. And if Gougan is our key to reaching Nantaje, and he's almost always off wandering in the hills — "

"I'll start immediately, Colonel. But about dinner with the Frye couple at their house — "

"I'll make your apologies. Perhaps you'll be able to drop by later."

"And maybe not."

Marcus Cavanaugh turned his steps, and moved as fast as his two long legs would carry him. The sutler kept his store and drinking premises both at the opposite end of the fort. Marcus entered the low adobe building and was in familiar territory amid high-stacked hogsheads and shelves. Row upon row of small tobacco sacks were flanked with airtight cans of peaches, tomatoes, and meat. Combs and shoelaces lay alongside bars of soap. Neck kerchiefs hung from wall pegs.

Since the trumpeters had not signaled duty dismissals, the place was empty, but for a single clerk. Marcus brushed down the aisle, his saber scabbard rapping boxes and barrels, until he found himself in the officer's bar. He recognized Lieutenants Quint and Scallery huddled over beers. The atmosphere was mostly free of flies — and not too hot. Sweating *ollas* swung from cord nets near the customers' heads. Water evaporating from the massive clay jars cooled the surrounding air.

"He's at the enlisted men's bar, then?" Cavanaugh demanded.

"Go on in, if you think you can stand the smell," Scallery told Marcus.

The major plunged through the narrow connecting door and was greeted by an awesome sight. One of the largest human beings in Arizona Territory spun to face him, and as he did so, he drew himself to full six-foot-eight height and stretched. Harry Gougan was clothed in buckskin and wore a full beard and long matted hair the same rich, brown color of bear fur. Even the giant's gait was strangely grizzlylike as he shambled forward.

"Marcus Cavanaugh, by the saints and their mistresses!" The big man flourished a whiskey bottle. "My nemesis of old! Can you not leave a man to drink his coyote piss in peace?"

"Now, gents — " the sutler behind the bar began.

"Button yer trap," whooped Harry Gougan, contorting his long-jawed face. He put the bottle to his thick lips, drained it, and hurled it aside.

"Powder River, and let her tear!" the giant whooped. And Harry Gougan launched himself at the major with both fists sledging.

Chapter Five

The man in buckskins moved quickly for one so large, but Marcus Cavanaugh's reflexes were honed and sharp, and he was able to dodge the first onslaught. Gougan's fist missed its mark, the officer's chin. The human mountain hove about, reeling, and lashed out again. This time his moccasin-wrapped feet tripped over each other, thanks to the whiskey he had consumed, and he skidded into the pineboard bar. The frightened sutler crouched against the bottle-laden shelves, afraid to interfere.

The sounds of scuffling brought the officers in from the other room, and with them a couple of privates who'd put in an appearance. A command was snapped.

"Men, help out the major!"

The two privates, both of them young, peach-cheeked, and new to the garrison, moved forward, hesitating. Even outnumbered, the buckskinned stranger looked an adversary they'd do well to beware of.

"Harry Gougan," Marcus Cavanaugh called flatly, "You don't really want this trouble, do you?"

"Damned bluebellies!" The hairy giant launched himself at the nearest private, Matthews, and propelled him back into the wall. "Orin! Help me!" the poor young soldier cried.

The second green trooper rushed in rashly and received a fist in the face for his efforts. But this one had been a brawler back on the farm. He countered with a punch and connected with the big man's chest.

"You call that a blow, youngster? Take this!" Gougan's enormous arms flexed. He grabbed Orin with his steel-trap hands and flung him. By this time, Private Matthews had returned to the fray, flailing wildly. After a few ineffectual hits, he jumped on the giant's back and circled his throat with an arm. The wiry elbow was buried in dense facial brush, but Gougan only laughed. He shrugged. Private Matthews's hold was broken. The trooper swung over the giant's head and hit the floor.

"I'm a curly wolf!" Gougan bellowed. "Try and lick me, and you're gonna meet your end!" His fierce eyes fixed on Scallery and Quint. There was a quiet scrambling, and a table was thrust in Gougan's path. Marcus Cavanaugh decided it had gone on long enough. He stepped behind Gougan, clutched a bottle from the bar, brought the missile up and around in a neat, tight arc. Hard glass met the hair-matted skull decisively. Harry Gougan's knees buckled and he started to collapse. "Grab him!"

The junior officers moved fast, catching the huge, slack form, and momentarily supporting it.

"Here! In this chair!" Marcus ordered. The lieutenants sat him roughly down.

The major stood over the unconscious man, until the massive face twitched and his eyelids flickered. "He'll come around in a minute and be all right. I'll handle things from here, lieutenants. You can go back to those beers. Oh, and on your way, tell those privates to clear out."

Within seconds, Marcus and Gougan were alone in the grubby sutler's barroom.

"I heard you were here and only came to try and talk," Marcus told the recovering man.

"Palaver! Screw it!"

"This, from my one-time best white scout?"

"Them days, Cavanaugh, they're damned well over! Now stand clear and let this hairy buffler shake himself."

The massive man did so, in the manner of a rain-wet dog.

"There. I'm a mite soberer. Now I'd best be shaking the dust of Bowie. I've bought me the stock of rifle rounds I come for. Time to head back for my spread." With a floundering of limbs, he climbed shakily to his feet.

"I want your help with something." Marcus sensed he'd better speak up quickly. "A meeting with Nantaje." Gougan's head swung about, bushy brows raised in mild surprise.

"I don't work for the government no more. Just run me a few cattle in the hills."

"Allowed to by the redskins, who'd kill any other settler in those parts, or at least run them out." Marcus stood toe-to-toe with the taller, broader man. "Harry Gougan, you know why they're letting you be."

"Sentagolatha." The big man nodded, looking down for a moment.

"The woman you're married to. Nantaje's own sister!"

"He's a pretty mean feller," Harry Gougan grumbled. "Nantaje. The few occasions I been in his company, I seen the hate of white folks nigh boiling over. Claims he's got the right to hate all whites. A spell back, a pack of ragtag militia slaughtered his squaw and young uns."

"Yes, a long time before this fort was built. That's been quite a few years. These days, most of the Apache people keep a kind of peace. Accept the terms of Cochise's treaty, stay on their own land, and take the government's allotments of blankets and beef."

A scowl. A shake of the bearded head. "The Injun broncos, they don't cotton to any of that. Cochise died in his wickiup. They claim the treaty's dead, too. Nantaje — "

"Yes?"

"I'm heading to my spread now. Bought my bullets 'cause ain't no other place to buy 'em. Made the mistake of running into you."

Marcus nodded crisply. "I'll ride on back with you and talk with Sentagolatha. If she wants the bloodshed ended, she might be willing to help. I want to meet Nantaje. I want to negotiate."

"If I allow it."

"Just let me ask her. Give me time to have a horse saddled and change from this dress uniform."

"Them fancy duds do make a feller want to laugh."

Inside half an hour, Major Cavanaugh, with Thornhill's permission, joined Gougan outside the fort's west wall. It was full night, and the moon glowed through drifting clouds. The scattered cactus and Spanish bayonet on the flat shone silvery pale. "We'll be riding almost till sunup," Harry Gougan offered. "Major, you settled good in that ass-breaker of a McClellan?"

Marcus grinned and muttered, "Forward ho."

"You're really a hell of a feller, Cavanaugh. I ain't forgot that time you saved my bacon in a raid. But with a belly full of sutler's whiskey afore, I just — "

"Forget tonight."

The horses' shoes crunched on the gritty desert hard-pan. After a while the high clouds scattered to show hard, bright stars.

Because the full brunt of summer had not yet come to the foothills of the Dos Cabezas, the night was free of moaning hot wind, and not particularly unpleasant for riding. Man Mountain Gougan's route led him and Marcus steadily toward higher ground, and after two hours in the saddle, the officer found the landscape dramatically changed. He knew the daytime aspect of the country, when it looked increasingly wild and forbidding, with rugged peaks cleft by canyon cuts. Still, under gentle moonlight, it all seemed softer and less hostile in its appearance, if not in fact.

The officer forced his eyes to stay alert, roaming along the enclosing slopes that were studded with cacti, agave, mesquite. He discerned nothing that moved, and knew Gougan, with his trained scout's savvy, would be the one to sense danger first. As the men continued to urge their horses upward, they arrived at a canyon mouth, lofty-walled and looming. The going became tortuous, zigzagging, and the men could no longer ride abreast. Gougan took the lead and the man's broad form became a shadow among deeper shadows.

Marcus Cavanaugh let himself be guided by the scraping sounds ahead, wooden stirrups against hard granite. Then the close walls fell away suddenly, and they came to a stream. In the season ahead the clear waters would be dried up, but tonight thirsty men and mounts might take take a drink. Gougan reined in and climbed down, Marcus following suit.

"Not much farther, now."

The man mountain had turned less talkative the closer they came to his wilderness home. That was all right with Marcus. Just so long as there'd be no interference later, when he tried to make his point with Sentagolatha.

The major knew that reaching Nantaje through his sister was going to be difficult. But the alternative would be not reaching the war chief at all.

At last, the rising sun at their backs tinged the sky a pale pewter hue. The two men gigged their mounts from the last cedar break and across a small, grassy swale. At the far end, with granite outcrops looming overhead, was a cabin of unpeeled logs. From a stone chimney came a smoke wisp. Harry Gougan stepped from leather, threw laden saddlebags over a massive shoulder and stalked toward the structure.

"Sentagolatha! I'm home!"

The door swung open on rawhide hinges and the woman emerged. Wearing a near-white deerskin dress, she was slim and raven-haired and she moved as gracefully as a fawn, slowly at first, and then breaking into an eager run. She threw herself into the big man's arms. "Harry!"

Remarks were exchanged in a strange tongue, the words of which were slurred and sibilant, and then the woman peered past her husband at the Army man as he dismounted. The pretty, coppery face with wide, black eyes became impassive. Finally Gougan gestured Marcus forward.

"Sentagolatha, you recall Major Marcus Cavanaugh from over Bowie way. He ain't never one to mean us no harm. Now try your white folks' talk on him, gal."

"Good day, Major Marcus Cavanaugh. As my husband's friend, you're welcome here." Her English had improved a lot since Marcus had seen her last. Of course, that had been months before, on the last visit she'd made to the fort.

"Pleased," Marcus said.

"Fix us breakfast, gal, whilst we unsaddle and turn the broncs to graze."

She turned and walked inside. Gougan muttered glumly in his beard. "Pretty little thing. Hate to see her get upset."

"I'll try not to upset her badly," Marcus vowed.

"Bring up Nantaje, and bad upsetting can't be helped."

When they'd hung their saddles on the pole corral's fence, they rubbed the animals down with handfuls of grass. By then it was bright morning in the high country. Marcus was enjoying the bird calls and the flitting feathers he caught sight of in the brush. "Come on, then," Gougan finally said. "Let's go grub up."

In the cabin, hot food waited on battered tin plates on a crude table: bacon, fresh pan biscuits, and coffee in tin cups. The coffee was scalding and strong. Marcus complimented the cook.

"Thank you," Sentagolatha said, the large dark eyes cast down modestly.

"Wife," Gougan burst out, "the major, here, he didn't ride all the way from the fort just in hopes of a feed. He's come to jaw a mite with you."

"With me?"

"Go on ahead and do what you got to, Cavanaugh," Harry Gougan said.

Marcus began speaking softly and seriously, and didn't stop when the Chiricahua woman's black eyes widened. There was no interruption from the husband and wife, and he talked for a good long time.

"I do not think what you say is possible," Sentagolatha said when Marcus finally stopped. The major had fixed her with a questioning stare. "Nantaje, though related to me by blood, never minds what I say. I am a woman. I am a woman who left her people to take the white ways."

"Sentagolatha, I believe Nantaje will pay attention this time. Certainly more attention than to a message relayed by an Army man. Say it's more important than ever for him to make peace while he can. That the reservation Apaches of other tribes will join in hunting him. That they will do so in order to save their own lands."

"Nantaje, he hates the White Eyes. He will keep killing them whenever he can for as long as he lives. He has sworn this."

"Get this message to him. Major Cavanaugh will deal firmly, but be fair. The renegade chief will be treated like a surrendering foe. If he raids more settler camps, though, to slaughter and torture, and abduct white women and white children, it will be too late. Then Nantaje will be declared an outlaw. Then he will be hunted down and hanged."

"To the red man, the white man's hanging is a shameful death."

"I know."

Marcus glanced at Harry Gougan, but found his flat face unreadable. "Well, Sentagolatha, will you try to get your brother word?"

"I will try. I make no promise of what might happen."

"I'd never ask you to promise."

"Well, there's work to get done around this place," the mountain man put in. He slammed his floppy slouch hat over his eyes, and rose. "Got to go shooting after meat, ain't that c'rect, gal?"

"If it's meat you wish to eat, not berries, my husband."

"I'd better be going now," Marcus said.

"That's true," Harry Gougan observed.

Two team-drawn Conestoga wagons crawled across the

desert flat, moving more slowly than sluggish snakes. Canvas bonnets flapped lazily in the listless breeze, and the drivers shuttered their eyes against blowing grit. Noontime pale, the sun's fierce disk slammed the land with furnace heat. Although the mules in the traces didn't flag, the ridden horses did.

For the second time in a quarter mile, the mount carrying Luke Tyler stumbled. The Ohio-bred sodbuster spit an oath out under his breath. He wished he had saliva enough to really spit, but saving canteen water, he hadn't drunk a drop since breaking camp. That had been at dawn, six hours ago. Now his mouth felt blotted dry, as if with new wool flannel.

Tyler's glance stole to the bulky lead Conestoga, where his brother Lem slouched on the hard ash seat. Beside him, Lem's wife Ida and their son rocked and jounced. The son was at his mother's breast. On the wagon behind the seated dust-eaters were Luke's pregnant wife, Abby, and the Tyler boys' sister, Charity, buxom at sixteen. Abby was doing a good job with the reins, Charity a good job keeping a lookout. Her brothers had taught her to shoot, and an old but cared-for Henry carbine rested in her lap.

This was said to be Indian country, although the party had yet to see a single reddish skin. The most formidable enemy right now seemed the desert and the thirst. Lightening the load yesterday of the families' furniture had helped. The toads and tarantulas would have their pick of discarded extra clothing. But the going was still slow, the western peaks were days off. And who knew what they'd find there? Luke Tyler swore again.

He gigged the animal he straddled toward a nest of naked hills that lay in the party's path. The bowllike sink that they were crossing was about to be left behind. The settler studied the broken ground through the shifting veil of haze. Maybe there'll be a seep, he thought, though it was a dim hope. Water usually was signaled by greenery, and he could see nothing green. The roan stumbled again. The man kicked the sweating flanks.

"Ride on ahead, Luke! Scout the trail!" Lem called up to him.

Before the rider could act, they heard a closer, more frightening yell.

Over the hump rode a band of men on runty ponies, their black hair wild and free but for colorful headbands. Shirts of hide covered their squat, muscular torsos. Strong-planed faces were daubed with stripes of pigment. More than a dozen in number, some brandished rifles, some bows and arrows. As they pounded near, shrill whoops gave way to gunfire. Luke Tyler reined the bay about and gave hard spur.

He was nearly back at the abruptly halted wagons when his horse took a slug and went down.

"Come on, Luke! Run!" came Charity's panic-stricken cry. The man rebounded from the dusty spill, pumped his legs as best he could and covered ground. Now a flurry of shots broke out ahead, and he knew he was getting covering fire. Still, at his back sounded a grim thunder. The mounted Indians were gaining, as they surely must. Just a few more steps, though, and he'd be shielded with his kin.

Luke's left knee exploded in agony, and the settler pitched headlong. Over and past him the savage horseman rode, their shots directed beyond the crumpled form toward the other whites. Lem moved quickly to align the wagons side by side, and he and Charity struggled with the harnessed teams. As they did so, the paired sisters-in-law each worked a rifle that she trusted. Ida, the older woman, had placed her baby beside her on the ground near where she'd stretched out flat.

An Apache bullet spanged dust in her frightened blue eyes. The child was bawling pitifully. The mother took a shot to the face that blew her pretty jaw off. Blood splashed the infant, who simply wailed on.

Off to the right, Abby found a target. She triggered, and a brave grunted, dropped, and lay still.

On his feet at the head of a struggling mule, Lem Tyler jerked in pain. An arrow struck the man's shoulder and spun him, hurling him over the wagon tongue and down. He fisted his six-gun and tried to rise. One steel-tipped shaft found his chest, and then a second. But he was not to perish by arrows. The bright tow head burst at a bullet's impact, splattering crimson and gray from his brains.

"No! No! No!" shrieked Abby Tyler. Apaches were leaping from their plunging ponies and dashing in close. Abby fired her Henry and missed a charging, dodging redskin. The unscathed target grabbed her gun and laughed. His strong hand wrapped in the woman's hair, and she screamed. She was kicked in the stomach. She felt her unborn baby twitch in the womb. She screamed again.

Meanwhile, young Charity strove to pull herself aboard a mule. The panicked animal, wrapped in its harness, plunged and sunfished and kicked. Charity lost her seat and fell heavily. She rolled into a ball at the feet of a running redskin. The raider dropped on the slight female with both knees, and drove the breath from her lungs. " Oh! " she squawked. Then she was drawn up by steel-trap-tight arms, forced to breathe her captor's stench.

The Indian locked fingers in the girl's neckline and jerked downward. He stripped her dress off as if shucking corn, and she spun away, fragile and naked. By this time all the surviving Tylers had been stripped — including the babe. A painted buck took the infant by the feet and bashed its head against the wagon bed.

The two naked women shrieked anew. Both were being dealt their own harsh pain. The pregnant Abby was knocked down, and a stocky buck who'd lifted his breechclout aside dropped between her thighs and began a brutal pumping. For her part, the woman lay limp and without life. Luke, with his shattered leg, was dragged up and tortured with hard kicks.

The leader of the bronco band was not tall, but he had an impressive build. Under his dingy headband his face was stony, his downturned mouth like a slash from a viciously wielded knife. The single broad stripe of war paint across cheeks and nose made him doubly terrifying. Now he moved near the girl Charity and raked her nakedness with dark eyes. He growled an order, and she was tossed across a pony's back. An agile buck leaped quickly up and held her tightly. She heard a name grunted. *Nantaje.*

But she was helpless and couldn't move.

Again the leader snapped a brisk command, and one of the bucks ran up flourishing a knife-tipped war lance. Strongly, remorselessly, a burly Chiricahua drove the point through Luke Tyler's chest. Skewered, the hapless white man was pinned to the earth. More braves gathered like coyotes at an elk's corpse, and several helped to drive the spear deep in the ground.

The impaled settler screamed and writhed as the Apaches leaped to their ponies' backs. Then the leader kicked his into a swift gallop, the others at his heels. The withers of her captor's mount dug Charity Tyler cruelly in her belly and breasts, but she bit her lip and held still. The raiding party surged across the malpais land. She wished she were dead like her kin.

Chapter Six

Fort Bowie baked in the colossal oven that was the desert day, a clutch of structures under a brassy sky, a dusty quad locked by looming gray adobe. From the sprawl of the buildings and the Indian scouts' wickiups outside the walls, smoke from cook fires whispered upward in threadlike strands. It was hours before the descent of hot nighttime winds from the hills. Troopers knew it. Scouts knew it. Even the washerwoman wives of soldiers down on soapsuds row knew it.

The off-duty scouts and the females rested, trying their best to stay cool. Irritable noncoms barked languid orders. Drilled men shambled through perfunctory paces. Officers swore.

From the gateside parapet, sentries surveyed surrounding flats and knolls. Private Hotchkiss and Private Penrose strolled close and exchanged low words. Theirs was a dull job, drenched with sweat, and occasionally a man needed to talk.

"Did you hear about the brawl last night?" Penrose's mouth curled in a smirk.

"Aye. And who ain't?"

"Not ever' day a major'll take a hand hisself."

"Bloody right." Hotchkiss's cockney accent grated the eardrums, but it was better than silence.

"Oh, old Cavanaugh's knowed to do the like. Take the lead in battle, too."

"Orin claims the drunk mountain man was seven foot tall."

"More like six and a half. But it turned out them two were friends, after all. The major and the beard left the fort together. Corporal Stiles, he seen 'em ride out, close as ticks on a hog."

"Stiles, he'll drill a troop worse'n a brass-balled bastard!"

"I hate the son of a bitch, too."

The approaching rider had drawn near unseen, and now he let out a weary call. "Sentries! Open up!" And when they peered over and down, Penrose and Hotchkiss both gulped.

"Christ, it's him, the old man!"

"And we didn't hail him. He hailed us!"

As soon as the gates were swung wide enough for the rangy bay, the officer rode through. From the misery-giving McClellan, Marcus snappily returned the proffered salutes. "Penrose and Hotchkiss, aren't those your names, privates?"

"Yessir!"

"You two men are on report!"

Leaving the pair standing open-mouthed with their Springfields in hand, Marcus trotted his horse across the parade. In front of regimental headquarters he swung down stiffly, handing the reins to the private who waited beside the steps.

"Colonel Thornhill, he's inside?"

"Yessir!"

Marcus handed the man the reins and ordered him to take the horse around to the post paddock. The bone-weary major strode up onto the veranda and through the door.

The commander was just returning his flask to his desk drawer. "Oh, Major, it's you. Frye's gone over to the quartermaster's about some requisitions." He returned Marcus's salute casually. "So you're back from your ride over to Gougan's ranch. You must be thirsty."

"I can eat and drink my fill later, Colonel. If I might make my report?"

He told about his journey, of Gougan's pessimism and Sentagolatha's fears. Nantaje wasn't likely to cease his raids, the bearded giant and wife were convinced. Still, the war chief's sister had promised to pass the word that the bluecoat officer called Cavanaugh wanted a parley. Marcus finished his narrative with a question. "Colonel, is treating with the renegades so important as we thought?"

"More so than we thought," Thornhill said grimly. He peered at his executive officer with liquor-pouched eyes. "I spoke with Hiram Titus again before he left Bowie, and the Bureau man was damned sour. He doesn't understand or much want to understand our point of view, Major. Nor does he share the fear of what a united Apache nation would mean."

Marcus's face fell into a mask. "It makes a thoughtful man wonder, Colonel, where insensitivity or stubbornness leave off and where greed begins. Titus and that Pearson fellow struck me as being hand in glove, somehow."

"That railroad man, like many of his breed, seemed a predatory wolf. He's backed by powerful Eastern money. The kind that politicians respect."

"Or the kind that Hiram Titus might like lining his pocket with?"

The colonel's head snapped around. "Strong words, Major. Very strong words. What you're suggesting — "

"I'm suggesting only that no public interest whatever is served by an Apache war. You know that, and I know it. As it stands, the raiders that are troubling us — Nantaje's Chiricahua renegades — are as much outlaws to the other Apaches as to us. By tarring all Apaches with the same brush, we'd only unite them in an all-out fight against us. That kind of hell Arizona can't bear."

"There'd have to be heavy army intervention made then," Thornhill replied. "To try and take Nantaje in the wilderness strongholds."

"Would the government be willing to commit troops then? We're as short-manned as sin right now."

"Unless — "

The two officers' gazes met. After a short pause, Marcus was the first to speak. "The affair smells, Colonel. I don't doubt Titus and his political clan take bribes. The Army's keeping us hamstrung for want of troopers, allowing the district to erupt. Then, when extermination becomes the policy, the generals will throw in men, cannon, Gatling guns. Damn!"

Footfalls rattled out on the veranda duckboards. "Quiet," the colonel hissed. "Keep your suspicions to yourself. Here comes our adjutant."

Captain Shelby Frye sauntered in. His tender skin had reddened, as usual, in the heat. The desk soldier was fatigued. "Tiresome paperwork," the thin lips grumbled. "Fouled up quartermaster's records. Oh, Major Cavanaugh, it's you. Back from your little mission, I see."

"Yes, Captain, I've returned. Now, Colonel, I'd like to change out of this dress uniform." Marcus saluted, and the colonel saluted back. As he was leaving, he heard Frye discoursing on supply matters of one kind or another. He sauntered the boardwalk toward "officer country," thinking about horses, weapons, men, and what could be done if he only had enough of them.

Day followed monotonous day at Fort Bowie. As the summer set in, the men endured a grinding routine. There were the morning and afternoon drill periods, mounted and dismounted, and even through-and-through cavalrymen who loved riding grew sick of the two-hours-per-day, six-days-per-week sweat. Veteran horses learned the drill commands as well as soldiers. When a careless private fell off, his mount would keep formation for the rest of the exercise. Such was fodder for talk in the sutler's barrooms evenings, before "Call to Quarters." Nightly, the fiery whiskey distilled in Tucson — dubbed Old Commissary — flowed as plentifully as from a well. An alcoholic haze encompassed the privates, the noncoms, and all the officers but a strong firm-minded few.

When the supply wagons rolled in short of requested ammunition for the fifth straight time, Major Cavanaugh canceled all schedules of company target practice. Small-arms rounds were too scarce to expend, other than at enemies. The remount vendor from over Camp Grant way brought in a herd, and for a week there was excitement in the paddock, breaking the new horses to saddle.

All, even the post washerwomen, ate, slept — lived — according to the bugle calls. Reveille blew at 5:30. The first drill took place at 6:15. Fall-out for fatigue duty commenced at 8 o'clock, to be followed in half an hour by the mounting of the guard. The roasting afternoons were spent in additional fatigue, the absolutely needed duties that kept the post going. The stables had to be shoveled and swept, wood gathered from surrounding countryside for cooking, equipment oiled and kept fit and polished. Some proud soldiers' jobs were maintaining the several fire-fighting pumper engines. Others toiled at painting and carpentry on the grit-scoured buildings.

Sundays meant a few breaks in the round. After "Church Call" and a sermon from the chaplain, those lucky men who hadn't drawn guard duty had some hours of free time. Mouth organs and concertinas were pulled from kits, but mostly there was plain, hard loafing. Some of the officers' wives arranged picnics of a sort, but never too far from the fort's protection. Colonel Thornhill had laid down that rule, and Marcus concurred. So, under greasewood clumps on knolls a stone's throw from the wall, picnickers made do. Women in neat bonnets and dresses played and made merry with offspring. Husbands, as often as not, seemed less than comfortable. They may have been anticipating their next outing on patrol.

The patrols were usually hell. Trotting out in that first heated morning light, the men's bellies and canteens would be full. The rested horses might even be inclined to frisk. But then a businesslike grimness would set in. They were out there to do a dirty job, these riders in the thin, blue columns. The Chiricahua renegades under Nantaje were some of the most fearsome warriors in the world, as viciously cruel in their battling and its aftermath as any. Their practice was to deal death without mercy. And God help any who fell into the savages' hands!

The broncos' chief enjoyment was in their treatment of wounded enemies. This was what the cavalrymen had been told and shown again and again. The veterans had seen too many staked-down human remains, buzzard-torn but tortured first, the most hideous deaths imaginable. The only prisoners that these raiders took might be young women. And chances were that the hapless females would have preferred to die.

From twenty to thirty men strong, the scouting companies rode forth, although the War Department's Table of Organization posted correct numbers at about double that. From six to ten pack mules accompanied them, cared for by two packers. These hardy animals carried food, spare ammunition, and kegs of water. The water reserve was usually needed desperately. Sometimes *tinajas* — "tanks" — on the heights would be found unfilled by rain. In such cases, the trek back to the fort could be a thirsty one. Fifty miles of white caliche crust stretched in all directions, unbroken by any watercourse.

And always, by day, the fierce mailed fist that was the sun, kept hammering, hammering. And by night, they endured the howling, hot wind.

The regiment had lost Dutch Yancy, its premier white scout. Now the best scouts out of Bowie were their Apache scouts, Mescaleros, the age-old foes of the rival Chiricahuas. These scouts could reconnoiter from horseback or afoot, and the same went for fighting. They could shamble in the desert all the long, brutal day through and accomplish forty miles or more. This far outdid the mounts. And the Apaches drank mere thimblefuls. Their officer, Lieutenant Aaron Neel, valued them. Marcus valued them. So did Colonel Thornhill. Only Captain Shelby Frye spoke contemptuously of the "filthy red niggers." The desk soldier didn't appreciate their unwashed smell.

Second Lieutenant Quint took Company A out early in the month. No hostiles were sighted. First Lieutenant Durkey's Company B had similar poor luck. Captain Feversham's Company G ran out of water in the foothills of the Dos Cabezas range, but the casualties only amounted to alkali-lined throats and shrunken stomachs.

It was First Lieutenant Ben Nathan's troop that found the slain emigrants. The place was the sink east of Thunderhorse Mesa, that mighty, threatening, flat-topped pile. The party of two wagons had been hit, the conveyances burned, the animals stolen. The people, naturally, were one hundred percent dead, and buzzard-eaten. From the condition of the corpses and the arrows strewn in the vicinity, what had happened was fairly clear.

"Chiricahuas," Ben Nathan reported crisply. The tall, lean lath of an officer stood at ease before the colonel's desk, staring past the scoured features of Thornhill at the fly-specked wall. "So the scouts told me, and they're reliable. Those would-be settlers had nary a chance!"

Marcus Cavanaugh, standing to the side, scrubbed a hand along his jaw. His mouth was a bloodless taut line. At the other desk, seated rigidly, Captain Shelby Frye paid close attention, too.

"Go ahead with your report, Lieutenant."

"Thank you, Colonel. I must confess, sir, that the ugly scene's one that I can't get off my mind. We saw the vultures from miles off first, so we turned toward where they were swooping. We reached the site after a few hours." In a few concise sentences, the officer related the grim details. The skulls of the dead had been smashed.

Thornhill grunted. "Savage superstition. The Apaches think they're freeing the spirits of the dead so they can't seek vengeance."

Marcus nodded.

The eavesdropping Shelby Frye's face turned slightly green.

"Well, repeat your story to Lieutenant Scallery, Nathan. He takes D Company out tomorrow, and I'll be ordering him to range down that way. Nantaje seems to feel he must strike travelers before they reach Thunderhorse."

"To the Apaches, those heights are haunted," Marcus explained.

"Yes, sir. My scouts claim the same."

"You may go now, Lieutenant Nathan."

"Thank you, sir!"

Nathan's gratitude showed in his young, but weary countenance when salutes were snapped. Although he held himself ramrod rigid, Ben Nathan exited near the point of total exhaustion.

"Hell of a thing," Thornhill mused. "Those Chiricahua raiders simply strike like ghosts."

"Like the ghosts up in that rock pile called Thunderhorse?" For some reason Shelby Frye saw fit to snort a laugh. It was easy to ignore the desk soldier.

"As I was saying before Nathan arrived, Major Cavanaugh," Thornhill continued. "with regard to the dispatch rider that reached Bowie earlier, our luck seems to have just changed. We can be expecting two fresh companies of troops, and they'll arrive any day."

It was a bright spot in an executive officer's hard life.

"What do you know!" Marcus's lean face split in a grin. "From where were you informed, sir? Fort Grant? Fort Craig? Fort Marcy?"

"Er, a from bit farther away than that. Tell me, as a point of information, Cavanaugh, what do you know about the men called Buffalo Soldiers?"

"Why, about what every major in the country knows who's not officered among them." Marcus frowned in thought. "Soldiers of the black race. Four permanent regiments were organized after the War between the States. These were stationed in the West. Two of infantry, and two of cavalry. Segregated from the other troops. Led by white officers, naturally."

"Naturally."

From across the room, Shelby Frye broke in. "Naturally! Major, Colonel, I've had experience with the nigger units." The other officers looked up in surprise. "Oh, all right! Indirect experience. When I served at the War Department in Washington, I handled some paperwork. It's always seemed to me that ex-slaves should perform laboring jobs, not fighting ones."

"The paperwork that you handled showed this?"

"Actually, the evidence on that exact point wasn't conclusive. But my view still stands to reason, doesn't it, sir? How can red niggers ever be defeated by black niggers?"

Thornhill scowled. "Frye, aren't the monthly supply requisitions past due? Shouldn't you be over at quartermaster stores this afternoon?"

"Thank you for reminding me, Colonel. I almost forgot."

Once Shelby Frye had cleared out, Marcus asked the fort's commander point blank. "Your bringing up the matter of Buffalo Soldiers — that didn't happen to be just idle chat?"

The older man's gray head wagged. "No." The rope-veined hands folded across the colonel's lap.

"Major, the replacement units are damn-well needed as you know, but maybe Titus had a hand in this. We're being sent companies from the Tenth Cavalry, experienced troops, but black men. The officer in charge is one that I've heard rumors about. One Captain Jenks Wilcox. Ranked dead-last in his class at the Point."

"George Armstrong Custer ranked last in his West Point class."

"Custer, the buffoon among the Army's western-plains commanders! There you have it, Major Cavanaugh. I rest my case."

61

Chapter Seven

Nearly fifty weary and dust-caked Buffalo Soldiers rode through Bowie's gate two abreast, their pack train of mules trailing in the van. Kerchiefs that had once been bright cavalry yellow hung in wrinkled folds. Most campaign hats were deplorably slouched. It had been a vile trip across the desert in all ways. Many water holes were dried up at that time of year, and those that remained, the troopers had found, were foul with alkali. Horses had weakened from poor or nonexistent forage on the nightly stops.

These dark, hard men were seasoned veterans of the Indian wars on the northern prairies, yet most agreed they'd never suffered quite so much on a march as in these past few weeks. In the Arizona desert the sun's glare was the harshest ever. The wind-blown grit dug under clothing, into eye sockets and nostrils. Mouths turned brassy. Now the blue-clad column spread across the parade ground where the sagging flag hung limp.

A chocolate-skinned sergeant bellowed an order, and down the lines the men swung from their McClellans to stand stiffly and slap thighs with gauntlets.

Marcus Cavanaugh took it all in from the veranda on the headquarters building, and his eyes were disapproving as a Sonoran *zopilote* buzzard's. Not that the troops were undisciplined, exactly, but rather they moved with an offensive, careless ease. There occurred a lag between barked command and response that wasn't heel-clicking, snip-snap Army. He expected better, even after a long, tough travel go. Marcus's gaze sought the officer in charge, and locked on the stocky white man.

Jenks Wilcox, at first sight, seemed to justify Colonel Thornhill's dire predictions. Marcus studied the wrinkled and unbuttoned uniform blouse, wider-than-regulation hat brim, custom-made but scuffed and scarred boots. Even the twin gold bars on the captain's shoulder boards seemed tarnished, like the impression he made.

You never get a second chance to make a first impression, Marcus thought sourly. The two men were going to tangle. Marcus decided it might as well take place now. The spit-and-polish major descended the steps. His ink-black, shining boots lofted rooster tails of quadrangle dust as he strode forward a few steps. Then he waited, motionless.

The captain in charge of the newly arrived company gave his reins to an attending black private, turned, and approached. Marcus studied the sweat-runneled face. It needed a shave. It was as squarish as the major's own, and about as experience-worn, for the officers were almost of an age. But Wilcox's great hawk nose beaked so prominently as to make him a homely man. Marcus's frown skewed his own set of ruggedly handsome features. The officers exchanged salutes.

"Captain Jenks Wilcox reporting, sir. The arrival of the new E Company now assigned to Fort Bowie. A pleasure to join your garrison!"

"Welcome to the regiment, Captain. I'm Major Cavanaugh, the post exec. Colonel Thornhill, Bowie's commander, happens to be ill this morning, but he's assured me that he'll be around later in the day to greet you and accept your written orders papers."

"My men, they've had a hard trek across your infamous desert, sir. Permission to dismiss them to tend to their mounts and be shown their quarters?"

Marcus surprised Jenks by denying him. "As unorthodox as it may sound, Captain, I'd like to look the new troops over while they're still grouped together as they are. Oh, not a formal inspection, of course. Time enough for that tomorrow."

"I don't see — "

"Humor me, mister. Humor me."

The pair walked toward the new arrivals and their horses, the officers' striped pant legs matching stride for stride. Both were whiplash-hard men, neither carrying a gram of excess fat. Jenks, who was shorter and stockier than Cavanaugh, picked up his step, showing he could maintain an officer's bearing after all. Marcus began to have hope. They stopped in front of the bulky first sergeant, who barked to the troops.

"Ten-*shun*," he shouted in a voice like a rusted hinge. With a bit of shuffling and shambling, the line of blue fell in.

Marcus was aware of eyes upon him. Irregular. All eyes of troopers at attention were supposed to be fixed front and center. Here was something else to chew Jenks Wilcox about. But not at the moment. There was already enough on the plate of these Buffalo Soldiers.

"The *Cavalry Tactics* manual, Captain Wilcox, you're familiar with it?" Marcus snapped. "The details on the equipment each trooper's mount should carry? I want to see the insides of those cantle packs, — rations, spare horseshoes, cartridges. I want to see the hobbles and picket pins."

Wilcox's deeply tanned face suffused a darker hue. But he kept his calm. "Sergeant Meadow, this is an inspection. Inform the men so." In mere minutes Marcus had determined what he needed to. Plenty of non-regulation camp equipment, a noteworthy deficiency of orderliness. The men had the correct items in their kits for proper horse care, though. They knew their mounts could mean their very lives in battle or on march.

"Very well, Captain. I've seen enough. I'll have a man detailed to show these troopers the paddock, the farriers' and blacksmiths' barns. The black companies will be quartered in tents along the Fort's outer east wall."

"What about barracks accommodations?" As an afterthought, Jenks Wilcox added, "Sir."

"We'll discuss that matter later, and in private with Colonel Thornhill, Captain. But come with me now, please. I want a word with you first. Follow me to headquarters. The adobe structure with the white-washed veranda. You said the trip was difficult. You didn't mention encountering any hostiles."

"We saw no hostiles, sir. Just signs. The worst evidences were the poisoned seeps and wells."

"You'll find those come with the territory, mister, at just about all times when Nantaje and his broncos are on the raid. I'll see that some Apache scouts are assigned to your company. You'll find them invaluable in this country."

"I'm sure."

They reached the headquarters and plodded up the steps and through the door. Inside, Marcus took the large but uncomfortable desk chair. Wilcox stood easily in the front.

"You and your units are an important addition here, Captain," Marcus began solemnly. "We've been short-handed for a damn long time, and the fact has fairly hamstrung us. Our job here is the protection of the Apache pass between Dos Cabezas and the Chiricahua Range to the south and the west."

"I'm told some renegade bands have gone off reservation."

"That's the case. The broncos are a tough lot, Captain, and under Nantaje, a particularly formidable leader, they amount to pure hell at surprise strikes and slaughter. It's said this war leader's particular 'medicine' requires he leave no survivors where he raids."

"Sounds bad."

"It's so bad, mister, that it's going to take disciplined men to break this garrison's run of ill luck. That's every speck of discipline I'll be able pour on. Discipline is a fighting force's axle grease. Hatred or duty may be its fuel, but to win battles — or even skirmishes — it takes more than that. It's why your companies are going to need to shape up. They'll be starting regular drills tomorrow."

"Yes, sir!"

"Another thing, Wilcox. Soldiers need example, as well as orders to follow. You might mark that beside your quarter's bedstead with chalk. Men follow leaders into the jaws of death because they've set a fine example. You see my point."

"Yes, sir!"

"Your quarters are in 'officer country.' Sergeant Major Brody is right outside waiting to point your way. That'll be all for now, Captain."

"Begging the major's pardon?"

Marcus Cavanaugh was somewhat surprised. "Yes, Captain Wilcox?"

"Speaking of quarters, sir, I request it for my enlisted men. Tents outside the fort's wall, like on a bivouac? That hardly seems, well — "

"The army maintains many unwalled outposts throughout the West. Vigilance and sentries have kept them plenty secure. It's said morale's even better at those places. In the unlikely eventuality of an attack here, Captain, your Buffalo Soldiers will move inside to help defend. Naturally."

"It's as much a question of comfort as of danger, Major Cavanaugh."

A small smile crossed Marcus's lean face. "This post is always echoing with enlisted men's complaints. The barracks are ill-ventilated ovens, infested with bedbugs and lice. Most men desire to be permitted to sleep outdoors." Then the Major's gaze locked with his subordinate's. "But in this particular case, Captain, there's another issue. My guess is, you already suspect its nature."

"Mine are black-skinned troopers. The other squadrons at Fort Bowie consist of white men."

"Except for the Apache scouts, who dwell outside the walls, as well. We're practical officers, Colonel Thornhill and I, and the men under our command are afflicted with the same prejudices as the rest of the country. The situation is this. We're under pressure to end the Indian uprisings. We'll never do it if there's conflict among factions of our own troops."

"I agree, the race thing's explosive. I've seen some trouble at other stations, although nothing too serious. Leaves in towns have brought some conflicts when the soldiers were spit at. Or denied the privilege of drinking in the saloons."

"They'll be allowed in our sutler's store, and well served, Captain."

"My men respect me," Jenks Wilcox said, "and I've come to respect them. I've two winners of the Congressional Medal in those companies. Two."

"We don't rest on our laurels at Fort Bowie, mister. These companies are going to drill. Plus pass the toughest of inspections, and do it again and again. Yes, and engage the toughest savage enemies they've ever had to face."

"They'll get through it."

"We'll have to see, mister. We'll just have to see. Captain Wilcox, you're dismissed for now."

Across the terrain dubbed the great dish of fire, the raiding party had ridden for days. Now their weary ponies carried the Chiricahua broncos warriors off the white caliche flats and into higher ground. The hills fronting the distant haughty mountains reared to surround the riders. Ridges crested and innumerable small canyons slashed the broken land. The mesquite that grew rank on the slopes signaled a bit less bleached-bone aridity, but the sun still slammed the beetling granite outcrops from dawn to dusk. The frail, captive girl, Charity Tyler, sensed excitement in the Apaches — and definitely not the same kind that had followed the slaughter of her brothers and their wives.

From the back of the wildish buckskin to which she was tied, the girl watched fearfully. Yes, the savages were picking up the pace. The mounts smelled water up ahead, and had begun to snort and frisk eagerly.

And then they broke onto canebrake-grown flat, and she spied the stream. A great wall of red rock loomed beyond it, bastionlike. Small cedars and other green brush bristled amid the talus slopes at its foot. The Apache broncos leaped from their mounts' backs to run forward on moccasined feet. Men crowded in next to the drinking animals, dropped down on flat bellies to dip heads and quench their own thirsts.

All except for the member of the band most lustful toward the captive. This was not the cruel leader, the one called Nantaje, for although he'd raped her several times on the first terrible day, he'd grown increasingly aloof. The bronco who approached her now was an appallingly grotesque figure who years before must have been maimed by some powerful animal. From the ground beside the horse, he peered from the depths of his mangled face. The fierce eyes actually seemed to strike out at her. His blunt fingers worked a moment at her rawhide ankle bonds, till he was able to pull her loose and tumble her to the ground. Her wrists remained tied as she lay on the rock-strewn bank.

Terror was in her eyes as she stared up at him. The twisted lips of the Chiricahua were perpetually curled in a fierce coyote's sneer. The scarred, caved-in face grinned close, and a stiffened, but strong, right arm lashed out to slam her budding breasts. She flinched under the worn flannel shirt she'd been given to fend off the killing sun. The pain flowed outward from her chest, and her stomach heaved.

For a moment this pain was even worse than the steady ache that throbbed in her crotch.

All the bronco bucks had by now raped her, taking turns as the others pinned her to the earth. But none so often or so terrifyingly as this one with the hideous face.

Now he grabbed her pale blond hair, stretched her on the grass, fumbled down his breechclout. Charity Tyler stifled a scream. The Apaches' habit was to make it worse for her when she screamed. She held the outrage and pain inside her, snuffling softly.

She was learning.

Behind the violently bucking torso of the attacking monster, the other warriors gathered to take their turns.

Chapter Eight

Captain Jenks Wilcox studied the face in the mirror above the washstand in his room, taking note of the bluish hue on his cheeks and chin, even when freshly shaved. He found himself considerably more comfortable, nonetheless. Nor did he smell or itch so badly as on those last sweaty days of the desert march to Bowie. On the trip he had partaken of fully as many hardships as the enlisted men under his command, refusing a portable cot at bivouacs and bedding down under a thin tent canvas on the stony ground. He had eaten the same rations of beans and hardtack. He had plodded an equal number of miles afoot to spare a worn-out horse.

He might not be polished and showboat Army, but he was lean, smart, and tough. He'd found a way to make his men want to follow him through hell, if need be. And that way was to endure what they endured, and then some. He'd led the same bunch of Buffalo Soldiers for two years, up on the Dakota and Montana prairies. Thus far, neither had let the other down.

There'd been engagements with Crazy Horse's Oglala Sioux, Sitting Bull's Hunkpapa Sioux, and the most reckless and daring strike-and-run fighters of the plains, the Cheyennes under Spotted Lynx. In the small skirmishes and the larger battles, Jenks Wilcox's Buffalo Soldiers had created glory that had mostly gone unsung. Yet, in one encounter on the Yellowstone, the captain's mount had been shot from under him. Gone to ground in a shallow gully, he'd had his bacon saved by hard-shooting Corporal Hank.

On another occasion, Wilcox and Sergeant Labe Meadow rode to the rescue of their squadron commander, Light Colonel Abraham McGowan. They'd saved McGowan from the painted braves, as well as his bugler and his fat, sleek charger, Sheik. Meadow had sustained wounds in both legs, an arm, and a hand. But in the process he'd managed to singlehandedly kill eight redskins.

All in good time, the appropriate decorations were pinned on the heroes' chests. There had been ivory-bright smiles on the deep-brown faces, and later wicked glares thrown by whites in nearby towns' saloons. Some felt heroism had to do with skin color. Jenks Wilcox had never believed that. And he'd lived to see his viewpoint proven.

He took another fleeting glance about the bachelor room in Bowie's officer's row. The furnishings were spartan, which was good enough for Jenks Wilcox. His blouse was buttoned to go out, his shoulder boards were sponged. He jammed his best kepi atop his inky mane and strolled out into the night. The officers' mess hall was already crowded as the post's new captain selected and took a seat. There was fresh roast beef on the tables in large central platters, and some garden-soldier's cabbage and turnips, as well. Fare, it seemed to Jenks Wilcox, fit for royal stomachs. At the head of the head table Colonel Thornhill sat genially enough, flanked by Major Cavanaugh — "Brass-Balls Cavanaugh" to to the mind of Wilcox.

Up and down the tables, the officers engaged in chatter. Wilcox, though, was a naturally quiet man and kept mostly to himself. Those around him spoke of fiancées and whores they'd known, and the talk grew animated. Jenks Wilcox shoveled in food hungrily, keeping corrosive thoughts where they belonged — to himself. It was something to do with his command of Buffalo Soldiers, he supposed. He'd felt the coolness in the cavalry officers' manner when introduced to many of them that afternoon.

He had him a lonely life, but he'd brought it on himself, he knew. Heedless of lockstep regimentation, he'd always seemed to rub the Army against the grain. It went back to his time at the Point, where he'd excelled in studies, riding, and marksmanship, but fallen in a more important area. Ass-kissing had never been Jenks Wilcox's calling. And this thing they referred to as discipline seemed an overrated waste of effort.

A lithe figure slipped into the empty chair beside him, and grabbed a fork. He speared a biscuit from a platter and took a hearty helping of meat. Although Jenks Wilcox was occupied with his own thoughts, he heard the newcomer's gruff words plainly enough.

"Aaron Neel, I am, Captain, if I may introduce myself. In charge of Company F, Apache Scouts."

Jenks Wilcox glanced up and spied the gold first-lieutenant's bars on Neel's shoulder boards. He grunted an acknowledgment around a mouthful of bread. "I'm Wilcox, of course. The new companies of black cavalry."

"We ought to get to know each other well over the next few weeks, Wilcox. The nature of our respective commands suggests that, doesn't it?" Neel had a long,

72

freckled face capped by sandy hair, and a prominent lantern jaw.

Interest sparked in Wilcox's eyes. "It might just do us and our men some good, at that." He gazed at Aaron Neel intently and decided to sound him out. "It's hard for to me tell this soon, Lieutenant, about Brass Balls Cavanaugh's attitude toward officers in our position."

Neel's tight mouth opened in a grin. "I think the 'Brass Balls' name inappropriate here, mister. Marcus Cavanaugh is all right and fair, a damned good executive officer in a hot-spot post. His personal god is duty, to be sure, but even that's all for the best at this godforsaken hole, Fort Bowie. These Chiricahua renegades need defeating through strategy, and it's at strategy that this particular major shines."

"Not a desk soldier, hey?" Jenks Wilcox stroked his shadowed chin.

"Not in the least, Captain," the lieutenant of the scouts' company said. "If Cavanaugh takes a course of action, it's for some damn good reason, you may be sure."

Captain Jenks Wilcox took a long sip from his steaming coffee cup. Somewhat suddenly, he had grown quiet and thoughtful. Neel felt the change, and pitched in to some dedicated wolfing of food.

Privates Hannibal Bogg, Obie Hank, and Moses Early sauntered slowly along in the dark fort compound. The footpath stretched ahead through the deep wall-flung shadows, straight toward the sutler's saloon and store. Lamplight shone a cheerful welcoming glow through square windows. The three Buffalo Soldiers slapped each other's gallus-crossed backs and guffawed.

The trio passed through the splash of doorway light and stamped inside. The enlisted men's saloon was packed and noisy, the patrons a raucous and jostling

73

mob. Blue-bloused soldiers crowded the oblong confines, but most concentrated on the bar, the source of rotgut crackskull that smacked of Mexican peppers, and warm, evil beer. The stink of sweat mingled with the stink of spilled liquor, and both were stale and intense in the hot airlessness.

The Buffalo Soldiers had to do some elbowing to reach the bar, which they performed good-naturedly. Their mouths felt as dry as unginned cotton fresh from the boll. When they finally thrust their flat bellies against the slab pine boards, they called out for beer. Mildly foaming schooners were thrust in front of them. "A nickel a schooner," the sutler stated dully. "That'll be fifteen cents."

Early fished out the three coins and slapped them down. "Serve a free lunch here, do you?" He was chuckling even as he said it.

"If'n I did, it'd just be more hardtack."

The black men quaffed the amber liquid deeply, and sighed. "Good stuff."

"Outa my way, nigger," rasped a voice at Bogg's side, and the private felt his shoulder slammed. Bogg looked around quickly. His dark forehead was shiny with sweat.

"I reckon you got the right to some dragon piss, too."

"Damned right," the beefy white private snarled. "But there's somethin' 'bout the stink in this here place, all of a sudden. Smells like old turds! Buffalo turds!" The sutler quietly shoved a whiskey glass toward the man.

"Better take it easy, Phelps," the sutler hissed.

"The hell I do! These three buffler sojers, they smell like shit, I say!" Then he added slurringly to the black trio, "Don't you, niggers? Don't you smell like the very stinkin' chunks o' shit you are?"

Three dark faces turned impassive as if on cue. Obie Hank and Moses Early pivoted around, checking the best path to the exit. It was twenty feet of hostile territory. The length of the route was lined by curious, stiff-faced white men. But Hannibal Bogg didn't turn from the gent with the insulting mouth. Rather, he sized up the white foul-mouthed man, who was very drunk.

"You *boys* gonna admit you-all are shit? Hell, a 'Bama buck like me can tell! Smell a nigger pile of — "

It seemed to Bogg that any satisfaction gained wouldn't be worth the labor. Contempt wreathed his features, and at last he turned to leave. But the white man called Phelps erupted in a rage and brought his whiskey glass up and around swiftly. The stinging contents splashed Bogg's face. "Now, *boy* ! What ya say t' that?"

"Let me past, mister. We don't want no trouble."

"No?" Burly Kine Phelps launched a vigorous but awkward swing at the black private. Bogg shuffled and dodged. Then his own punch whistled through air.

There were excited shouts from the watching troopers.

"Goddamn, a brawl!"

"Both big sons of bitches, too! A goddamn dollar says ol' Kine Phelps'll do th' butt-kicking!"

The door abruptly burst open, and a voice bawled. "Ten- *shun*!" Sergeant Major Brody rushed in, his meat-slab features livid. Rattled, the troopers in the room froze motionless.

Major Marcus Cavanaugh stepped across the threshold. "That's enough, you men! I want this place cleared, and I want it now! Now move, damnit, move!"

Within minutes the enlisted men's saloon was emptied. Marcus and the sutler stood together in the middle of the littered floor. "Happen to be making your rounds, Major?" the wizened bald man wanted to know.

From the doorway, the sergeant major coughed a chortle. "You might say so, Doffmeyer," the officer said coolly. "It's the Buffalo Soldiers' first night on the post, isn't it? Best for the duty officer to keep his eyes peeled."

When the major and noncom had left him entirely alone, Karl Doffmeyer asked a question of the scarred bare walls.

"That Major Cavanaugh. Has the man eyes, then, in the back of his head?"

Harry Gougan and Sentagolatha sat at the table in their mountain cabin sipping after-supper coffee. The mountain man, for all his strength and size, was extremely tired. That morning he and the Indian woman had killed one of the steers from their small herd, then spent the rest of the day preparing the meat. They meant to use some for immediate eating and the rest for drying and the preparation of salted jerky. The man had toiled side by side with his wife because he'd wanted to. It wasn't the white man's way to leave the work for the woman, as was done by rancheria bucks.

Together they had worked with sharp knives to skin and eviscerate the slaughtered animal. Gougan severed the longhorn's broad head with his axe, then used the tool to split the carcass along the backbone into equal halves. They'd fried the liver up for lunch, for it was the organ most savory to the Indian taste — and Gougan liked it, too. He'd let the woman slice and wrap cut meat in muslin while he disposed of the offal in a neighboring arroyo. He filled a bucket at the stream, and they'd washed their bloody hands.

Sentagolatha had roasted a haunch on a fireplace spit, and they'd supped plentifully, accompanying the juicy, rare main course with biscuits and wild greens. The cabin became overheated from the fire, and in his chair the full-bellied giant slouched and dozed.

Gougan woke abruptly at the sound of the clattering pot lid, as his wife put away the coffee beans. "Time for bed."

"Yes, my husband."

"Turn the blankets down."

The sun had long since sunk behind the sawtooth peaks. No lamp had been lit. The sole illumination was from the hearth's low glow.

Sentagolatha husked: "Ready, my husband. Let me help you undress." He permitted it. He watched from under slitted lids as she let her dress drop, stepped out of her soft moccasins. She joined him on the bed that he'd built of peeled poles.

He fell atop her eager, supple body with a passion fueled by need. She drove up at him with fine, slender hips, firm rump and thighs. The pair merged with all their strength and drive, and the time was very good for Harry Gougan. At last, satiated, he fell into a deep doze.

Late at night, when the gibbous moon was high, he woke and found the place beside him empty.

So, she'd chosen her time and gone.

It had happened before, when the Chiricahua blood in her veins had pulsed and roared. There was a sense that sometimes called her to her people, and when the time came, she would go. She'd always returned thus far, and she'd told him often that she always would. Harry Gougan believed the woman who was his wife. He knew she loved him.

Now he lay and thought of Sentagolatha, thought of her on the trail to the rancherias below the Thunderhorse heights, where her war-chief brother dwelt and made medicine between his raids. Sentagolatha would relay a White-Eye major's words to the Chiricahua renegade leader. Marcus Cavanaugh's message would be delivered.

What happened after that depended on wily Nantaje.

Harry Gougan rolled over under the bedclothes and drifted back to sleep.

Chapter Nine

The company of Buffalo Soldiers, in their freshly sponged uniforms, snapped from attention into the stamping, wheeling movement of vigorous dismounted drill. Their Springfield carbines were planted firmly on squared shoulders, and their polished boots moved in precision, raising a fine gray dust. Abrupt shouts of command rang from First Sergeant Meadow's mouth. The marching cadence was clear as the squared columns formed, broke and reformed. "One! Two! Three! Four! Left! Right! Left R-r-r-right. Left, *right*!" The black troopers stamped to a halt, heels clicking, and the manual of arms was called.

The gray steel of the rifles' barrels gleamed with the flashy movement of the weapons. The brass-capped butts slammed the earth, the rows of men stood stiffly upright in place. Impassive dark faces stared straight forward. Overhead, from the parade flagstaff, the Stars and Stripes fluttered in a faint breeze.

"They look pretty good in my book," Jenks Wilcox told the noncom. In the officers' lexicon, of course, 'good' meant perfect in all respects. "That's an hour and a half on this parade-ground hell, Sergeant. You may dismiss 'em."

"Yes, suh!"

Meadow shouted yet another order, and the long rows of troopers fell out. Jenks Wilcox turned and made his way slowly across the quadrangle, intent on getting to his quarters, stripping from the blouse of sweltering flannel, and splashing himself with water from his washbasin. The inside of his kepi's sweat band itched atrociously, and his boots squished as he walked. But he wasn't meant to get past the headquarters without being hailed.

"Oh, Captain! Step this way, if you please?"

He didn't need to turn to look. The voice was familiar enough. In the roofed veranda's shade he came up on the waiting Marcus Cavanaugh, who peered at him sharply. The officers exchanged salutes.

"I've been keeping an eye on that bunch of men, Captain," Marcus said. "I must admit there's been improvement in their looks and actions, at least here on the grounds of the post. I suppose your own opinion is favorable for the drilling just concluded?"

"I admit it is."

"My own view happens to be, mister," Marcus snapped, "that they do appear to be coming around. But I've heard a rumor, Wilcox, that you personally have been chafing at the bit. That's understandable for an officer who doesn't enjoy sitting on his ass. Well, I have a duty for your company. You'll ride out with the men tomorrow."

Wilcox didn't bother to conceal his smile. "Yes, sir. Thank you, sir. A scout after Chiricahua war parties, sir?"

"Not quite," Marcus stated. "There's a town east of here, Captain, called Perdition Springs. Out on the San

Simon flats between Bowie and the river. Nearest stop to the fort on the stagecoach line. The place also lies on the main north-and-south route through this part of the Territory. The name of our game presently is supplies. We've got word by telegraph that our big shipment of the year has just left Lordsburg, New Mexico. Neither Colonel Thornhill or I want to lose the ammunition on those wagons."

"I see."

"I hope you do see, Captain. Because Fort Bowie will be relying on you. You're to meet the wagon train at Perdition Springs and provide it escort all the rest of the way here. Now, hostiles have the run of the area, and there've been herdsmen burned out, and even some stages chased. Nantaje's been known to split the force he heads, and send small numbers where he thinks there'll be small resistance mounted. What he might attempt against this train is anybody's guess. He's always seeking to steal more weapons."

"I'm sure that E Company can do a job for you and the colonel, Major."

"You're to move out after reveille and be at Perdition Springs two days from then. Expect a slower pace on the return trip here. I'm requesting Lieutenant Neel to provide you with some of his best Mescalero scouts."

"Yes, sir. Thank you, sir."

"And mister?" Marcus added.

Jenks Wilcox turned back to look.

"Good luck. I have a feeling you may be needing it."

Juan Gomez looked up from his saddle mending and studied the desert. The *ramada* outside his low earth dwelling cast a pattern of stark shade across the flinty yard. Along the shimmering ground the most notable feature to be seen was the most worthless, the outline of a brilliant blue lake. The crystal waters broke on horizon-wide beaches, miles away, and yet no distance at all, for the sight was a pitiless mirage. Off to the south where no waters seemed to lap, spinning cones of dust raced, skipping along to vanish suddenly, leaving empty the yellow flats.

The elderly Mexican ceased the doleful song he hummed, dropped the needle made from cactus thorn and his thick, inflexible thread. He scrambled from his tailor's crouch to stand, although hunched by age.

He thought he'd glimpsed a movement in the desert distance, animal or human, he wasn't sure. His pipe-stem limbs began to tremble uncontrollably. There was indeed a spire of lofted dust out there, and it was coming in his direction fast.

It had been years since the Apaches had seen fit to seek water at the sorry, strongly alkaline spring behind the adobe hut. That last time, Juan Gomez had his two brothers Jorge and Carlos with him to help defend the place. The men had concealed themselves inside and fired their rifles through the loopholes in the foot-thick walls. The earthen roof had successfully resisted tossed firebrands. In the end, the Indians had drunk their fill, watered their ponies, and given up their attempt to dislodge the bastioned riflemen.

Of course, the Apaches had made off with the few horses and mules belonging to Juan, Jorge, and Carlos, but the Gomez brothers were content that they'd managed to keep their lives.

Since then, one of Juan's *hermanos* had returned to Sonora and married a fertile woman who had born him many children to make his days happy. The other brother, careless after drinking an abundance of mescal, had died from a rattlesnake bite. Jorge was buried out back in a grave marked by a weathered shingle.

Now Juan, with effort, tore his thoughts from the past to confront a present danger. The cloud of dust he

82

spied was clearly raised by horses and they were drawing near. By lowering the brim of his huge sombrero, Juan peered against the glare, and the picture he got was frightening. A band of Apaches was indeed closing in on him. He snatched up the wicker-wrapped bottle of mescal from his feet and ran, huaraches flapping, into the dim interior and slammed the door.

He didn't like the way the door flopped loosely on its leather hinges, but he'd postponed the needed repairs, and there was no time to make them now. His gun, an ancient Enfield cap and ball, rested in a corner. Juan fumbled with bullets, powder, and patches, and eventually managed to load. By now the wild horsemen were circling the dwelling — he knew this from the drumming of hoofs that he heard through the walls. Juan Gomez swigged from his bottle, and felt the raw liquor burn its way down his gullet.

Then he stepped to a loophole and peered out.

One of the new Model 1873 Winchesters in the redskins' hands boomed flatly, and a .45-40 slug slammed the adobe. Flung mud bits stung the Mexican's cheek, and he felt a hot trickle of blood. "*Dios mio!*" he rasped. Now a rataplan of shots rang out.

Juan Gomez thrust his Enfield's barrel through a small and narrow loophole. He aimed at a painted bronco's chest and triggered. A shout erupted from the savage throat, and the redskin brandished his war club. The Mexican's shot had been a clean miss. And now the Apaches were dismounting and fanning out around the hut on foot.

Juan Gomez worked frantically to reload. He licked his lips and squinted his eyes. His gnarled fingers fumbled. He dropped first his bullet pouch, then the powder flask, then the gun. Sounds from above could be heard now. Feet in moccasins. They were trying to stomp through the roof. Juan could see feel some falling grit. He plucked the Enfield up again and worked the ramrod, forcing home a load.

The door burst inward from a sudden violent impact, and several Apaches poured in. The painted stripes across their cheeks and noses had micaceous sheens. Juan Gomez tried to turn his last shot on himself, but the Enfield was batted down to discharge harmlessly. Strong sinewy hands jerked the Mexican from his cowering posture, and he was dragged struggling into outside glare.

There were wolfish grins as the warriors shoved Juan to and fro. It was play to them, but the Mexican felt stinging blows. From the corners of his eyes he saw the *ramada* frame ignite, and spirals of smoke bloomed skyward. The savages were rounding up his stock.

At a loud shout from the raiding party's leader, the broncos seized Juan. This time they bore him across the gritty caliche, yards from his fire-swept home. "No!" he cried when he saw where they were heading. He struggled and squirmed anew. A carbine barrel to his greasy temple half-stunned the captive. He was thrown to the ground and stripped of clothing, then rolled atop a crusted mound ridden with tiny holes.

Brawny Apache arms grabbed the Mexican's wrists and ankles and yanked in four directions. The frail frame was pulled guitar-string taut, then the limbs looped with *reata* strands, and pegged down. The man's ribs were outlined like cage bars beneath his stretched, bare skin.

Across the skin, several pathfinders from the great ant colony began to explore. They liked what they smelled and tasted. Soon, columns of the fiery, stinging red demons were pouring from holes. Apache lips smiled wickedly. Apache moccasined feet kicked the anthill's crust to stir up the insects.

Juan Gomez regained full consciousness in a blaze of agony, and from his lips flooded a series of shrill screams. He twisted and bucked against his bonds, but the ants only swarmed and stung deeper. They seethed in streams over the writhing, shrieking man. He contorted and strained, and they bit and stung more. Never, Juan Gomez thought, had such torment been felt this side of hell.

Among the watching group of ten Apaches stood the untried warrior youth Cosotee, out from the rancheria on his very first raid. He'd positioned himself near the mighty leader Nantaje to achieve notice, but thus far it had gone to other, more experienced bucks who led stolen horses off, fired cabins, pinioned victims for torture. Now, searching the scowling features of Nantaje, it occurred to the boy that this time attention might really be bought. He hoisted his breechcout folds around his thighs and waded — in moccasins — across the anthill to the pegged-down man.

With swift slashes with his knife he sliced off the Mexican's ears. The screams of agony piercing the air redoubled, and the grinning Cosotee waded back across the spongy surface. He thrust the red-drooling ears in his waistband, and glanced toward the war leader.

Nantaje smiled.

As the pewter smear in the east signaled predawn, the stirring bugle notes of Reveille swept the confines of Fort Bowie. Within minutes the barracks and compounds were filled with hurrying, bleary-eyed men. The prior evening's bouts of drinking at the sutler's had been no worse than usual, but there were scores of aching heads. The latrines filled and emptied, and the mess halls accumulated a staying, waiting, gobbling crowd. As quickly as they were able, the Buffalo Soldiers of E Company gathered with field packs at the paddock and began saddling up.

Final checks of the shoes, bones, and hides of the mounts were made, each by the individual horse's soldier-master, for each trooper's duty was to care for his own animal. Some bonds of affection had been woven between some men and their beasts, but that was the exception and not the rule in the U. S. Cavalry. Most men cared for their mounts because they were responsible for them — to the expensive tune of almost a year's pay. If they lost their horse due to neglect, that amount was deducted. It wasn't a pleasant prospect for a fellow to dwell on.

"Boots and Saddles" for Company E was ringing out that morning well before the posting of the guard. The men swung to their McClellans and settled down heavily. Sergeant Meadow lined up the column. Finally Captain Wilcox trotted up on his sleek chestnut gelding and took position at the head.

He adjusted the campaign hat with the crossed-sabers insignia pinning the brim up on one side. It was precisely level across his smooth, tanned brow.

He raised his stocky, yellow-gauntleted right arm. "Forward ho-*oo*!"

The giant gates in the tall adobe walls were swung wide, and with a creaking of leather and a jingling of bridle chains, the blue-shirted column trotted through.

As the gates swung closed behind them, Colonel Thornhill turned to Marcus on the headquarters steps. "Buffalo Soldiers, Major. One day soon we'll be discovering how they act under fire. But let's hope it won't be on the present duty."

"The guns and ammunition supply wagons?"

"If they're lost, Major, we'll find ourselves in one stiff bind."

"They won't be captured by Nantaje, Colonel."

"You've that much confidence in this Company E?"

"Confidence both in the company," Marcus assured him, "and its officer. Captain Jenks Wilcox is going to make it in this man's army, after all. I feel it in my bones. Oh, he needs some seasoning, he's a diamond in the rough, but — "

A frown furrowed the post commander's brow. "Did you see his uniform irregularities this morning?"

"The pinned-up hat brim? The lightweight canvas britches? Those trousers are government issue, Colonel."

"For stable-cleaning detail! Major, I'm wondering about that man!"

Major Marcus Cavanaugh's face split in a wide grin. "I'm a spit-and-polish officer myself, Colonel, as are you. But I'm still able, once in a great while, to see the other side. On a march or a scout, it's one's ability that's finally got to count, that and his sense of duty. I decided to leave off riding Wilcox for a while. I decided that just yesterday."

The colonel let out a gruff "Harrumph." Then he raised his eyebrows and spoke with skepticism. "You do suspect Nantaje will strike that train."

Marcus's features were serious again. And his voice, though low, was steel-hard. "Let's just say that Captain Wilcox and his men could be in for a testing, and a severe one. A true baptism by fire."

"May the Buffalo Soldiers of Fort Bowie do this regiment proud!" Colonel Thornhill concluded.

Chapter Ten

In the boulder-flanked trails and the barrancas of the rugged foothills that she traveled, Sentagolatha, Indian wife to Harry Gougan, recognized familiar country. She had ridden a full day on the shaggy dun mare that she'd taken from her husband's pole corral, spent a night out under the stars, and now, late this second afternoon, was nearing her journey's end. She had already passed the trail branch where Harry Gougan had once found and saved her after a bad fall. It had not been long after that lucky meeting that the giant white man had taken her for his wife.

This was the country of the tzel-o-gay, a range of low but ruggedly mountainous upheavals, the highest feature of the land save for the lofty, sky-nudging peaks far to the west. In the upper reaches of that mightier, more haughty range resided the lightning god, and it was a place the Apaches avoided in fear. In those blue-hazed realms of majestic peaks and diving canyon-cuts, restless unavenged spirits were said to hover on this side of the Shadow Land.

FLINT
IF HE HAD TO DIE, AT LEAST IT WOULD BE ON HIS TERMS...

Get a taste of the *true* West, beginning with the tale of *FLINT* FREE for 15 Days

Hunted by a relentless hired gun in the lava fields of New Mexico, Flint "*settled down to a duel of wits that might last for weeks...Surprisingly, he found himself filled with zest for the coming trial...So began the strange duel that was to end in the death of one man, perhaps two.*"

If gripping frontier adventures capture your imagination, welcome to The Louis L'Amour Collection! It's a handsome, hardcover series of thrilling sagas by the world's foremost Western authority and author.

Each novel in The Collection is a true-to-life portrait of the Old West, depicted with gritty realism and striking detail. Each is enduringly bound in rich, Sierra-brown leatherette, with padded covers and gold-embossed titles. And each may be examined and enjoyed for 15 days. FREE. You are never under any obligation; so mail the card at right today.

Now in handsome Heritage Editions

Each matching 6" x 9" volume in The Collection is bound in rich Sierra-brown leatherette, with padded covers and embossed gold title... creating an enduring family library of distinction.

Harry Gougan had often insisted on the foolishness of these beliefs, but, nevertheless, the Indian woman was unable to shed them. Now, on her approach to the hidden strongholds of the People, the superstitions again rose powerfully in her mind. She peered around from the dun's back and scanned the terrain beyond the narrow, winding trail. Huge wind-checked boulders stood shoulder to shoulder to either side, many as large or even larger than the cabins in which the white men slept. The clefts between these grew thick with cedar scrub, and the smoother slopes in front were dotted with green agave.

Then she rode atop a ridge and stood before a broad, wild panorama such as might be visible to a hawk in flight. The desert was to her left, hundreds of feet below. Closer, and directly ahead, she gazed up the looming mesa known as Thunderhorse, another set of haunted heights. Very near loomed immense, sky-blotting outcrops, and the first tall pines.

She was nearing the rancherias of her childhood, and strong memories had started to grip her. The smoke of cook fires wafted in the woman's nostrils. The dun rounded yet another bend, and Sentagolatha heard herself called to.

"Where is the woman in the deerskin *ho-chee* riding?" came the low call in Chiricahua from the trees. Sentagolatha pulled back sharply on her reins. "She rides to the *Tsibrocay*, rancheria where dwells her brother Nantaje. She is Sentagolatha, the Fawn Who Drinks at Dusk. She has come again visiting in the country of her people."

There was a guttural exclamation of surprise, and then: "Ride on, war leader's sister."

The woman kicked her mare's flanks and trotted past the concealed lookouts. At the bottom of a grassed depression stippled with oaks and alders, a group of wickiups huddled. Small, walled with brush and roofed with hides, they would have been thought miserable dwellings by the whites, Sentagolatha knew. Yet she knew, as well, the coziness to the People of these traditional dwelling places, the interiors of which were furnished with soft, piled skins.

The paths between the wickiups were full of liveliness. Women cooked food at their little fires, old men lounged and chatted together, children played vigorously at the favored game of pole-and-hoop. If it had been nightfall, there would have been the throb of drums and dancing. In time of peace, there'd have been festive drinking of the People's *tiswin* beer.

This was not a time of peace.

Sentagolatha noted at once the absence in the village of the male warriors. The lookouts on the circling ridges were mere untried youths. Clumsily, they clutched repeating Winchesters and tried hard to look mature. The Chiricahuas paused in their activities to peer curiously at Sentagolatha. She trotted the dun to the central dancing circle, and slid gracefully to the ground.

"You are welcome at the village, my daughter," said an old fellow in sagging breechclout as he boldly sauntered close. He wore a painted shirt of animal skin. His flint-gray hair was capped by a headdress of woven eagle feathers.

Sentagolatha recognized Noohatacah, the *di-yi* or medicine maker. Such a greeting to an arriving woman told much of the status she yet retained. A female warrior before she'd married Harry Gougan and went to live with him, she remained the sister of the great war leader Nantaje. Nantaje himself wasn't present in the rancheria on this day. He must be out with his fighting men on a raid, Sentagolatha surmised. Well, she'd leave the message from Major Cavanaugh with Noohatacah, and the *di-yi* could pass it along. Then the officer of the white soldiers would have no cause to be troubling Gougan and Sentagolatha more.

When she had finished speaking, the old *di-yi* nodded solemnly. "I hear Sentagolatha's words," he croaked. By now his face had turned stern, almost malevolent, and the dark eyes glittered in the withered, seamed cheeks like chips of obsidian. "Noohatacah hears the words of the warrior-woman, Nantaje's sister. But is she really of the People still, this woman who has gone among the White Eyes? Now she brings messages that may mean betrayal. Why should Nantaje pay them heed? It is a time of war!"

"For many Apaches this is no war time," she retorted. "Many of the People live on the reservations, and the life is not too bad. Only where the land is harsh and poor, all the animals slain, is the Apache's life difficult."

Noohatacah started to expound. "The White Eyes tell the Chiricahua and the Mimbres man that he must scratch in the earth. The Papago, the Maricopa people, *they* scratch in the earth. The Apache, he is of the fighters!"

"And you say fighting people, the real People, must make constant raids." Sentagolatha nodded. "It is the ancient way. And it is the way of Nantaje my brother. Still, you will give him the white major's message, Noohatacah. The white major wants my brother to hear his words."

"The white major, and all the bluecoats, they will find arrows in their bodies. Or the bullets from our rifles, stolen down in Mexico. Now Nantaje means to steal more still. Many rifles good for killing many White Eyes."

The visit wasn't turning out a happy one. Some of the young bucks had wandered over to stare and listen to the woman and the shaman talk. It was clear that Noohatacah, the great *di-yi*, was growing angry. Word had been left by Nantaje that the *di-yi* should make his medicine undisturbed. Youths' fingers were restless on their Winchesters' stocks. Sentagolatha decided to take her leave.

"I am going now, Noohatacah. Nantaje must have the major's message, and you will see to that. Then Nantaje will himself know to test the major's words. So it must be."

"Nantaje this very day raids the soldiers' columns! Steals the horses, rifles! Kills the men, bashes in their skulls! Nantaje will ride back triumphant! There will be drums and dancing, as the warriors dance their great deeds! There will be much *tiswin* drunk!"

"Farewell, Noohatacah," Sentagolatha said. She bounded to her mount's back and reined the mare about.

The frail old man with the fiery eyes was still croaking words as the visitor rode out.

Maybe she would travel through the night to reach her husband's cabin sooner, Sentagolatha thought. Harry Gougan would be lonely for the young wife that he loved.

And Sentagolatha loved her husband in return.

"The supply wagons haven't reached Perdition Springs yet," Sergeant Labe Meadow reported to Jenks Wilcox. The noncom's gelding tossed its head as it came up beside the captain's steed. Froth strung downward at its mouth corners after the short lope out from town.

Captain Wilcox decided he needn't use his field glasses to study the small clutter of buildings through the haze. He recalled the place all too well from the stop he and the company had made on their march south to Bowie. Perdition Springs was one of those nasty places that might have been set down by a mischievous tornado, a few shabby buildings of adobe strung along a single street, the rest of the town's junky structures ranged higgledy-piggledy about the saucer flat. The two saloons were of the lowest sort, reeking of sweat and vomit and cheap trading whiskey. The general-merchandise store was somewhat larger, but abominably stocked with poor-quality supplies. There was a run-down blacksmith and farrier's shop, and an adjacent livery, but the horses were plugs.

Perdition Springs was a lot like the real perdition must be, Wilcox reckoned. The so-called town squatted against its heat-blasted desert backdrop like a heap of chuckwalla turds.

"Not arrived?" Wilcox asked, shifting in his saddle. He had learned he'd be more comfortable riding in the looser, stable-cleaning pants. "But they left Lordsburg on time — there's been no word over the wires otherwise?"

"No, suh," Labe Meadow said. "But if they got hit by Apaches, then there wouldn't be no word."

"Of course, what you say is true. Sergeant, tell the men we'll bivouac here." The officer studied the declining sun, mopping sweat from his brow with a sleeve. "Several hours yet till dark. Assign pickets and horse handlers. We'll just have to wait this out."

"We'll be eatin' dry rations again this evenin', suh?"

"I'm glad you asked, Meadow. Yes, on consideration, you can pass the word that we will. However — " He held up a finger. "Later on, a third of the men may go into Perdition Springs. I think that number's what the saloons can handle in addition to their normal customers. We could be camped here for as long as several days, I expect. All these Buffalo Soldiers will eventually get their turn."

"Yes, suh!" Meadow's grin was a white streak in brown skin. "I'll pick tonight's good-luck batch, and tell 'em."

"And send a man over to get my tent erected."

Within an hour, the cavalrymen had pitched camp. Neat rows of white tents dotted the hard, cracked earth of the sloping hillside. The stream that originated at the town's bountiful spring trickled below the site, and the horses watered there, downstream from some laughing troopers who filled cooking containers and canteens. Several campfires already lapped under pots of warming beans. Chipped-enamel coffee pots were also on the simmer, lofting their pungent fragrance.

Jenks Wilcox sat tailor-fashion in the shady shelter of his tent, attempting to bite into a regulation slice of hardtack. On a tiny camp table his tin cup resided, filled with strong-flavored, ink-thick brew. The officer's thoughts had wandered to the evening ahead and its promised tedium, and he had just about decided on a hike into Perdition Springs himself. There was a score to settle that had been hanging fire for a month, and he was anxious to see the matter through to its end. He heard his name spoken.

"Captain Wilcox, suh?"

He glanced up at the smooth black face of tall Private Cable. The enlisted man was holding aside the tent flap. "Buckboard comin' into the camp. Feller on the seat tells the sentry he's after you. Them are his words, captain. Said 'After you,' and his mouth it was set about as wicked as sin. Hell, he's rollin' up outside the tent just now!"

"A townsman? I wonder if — " Jenks Wilcox stroked the stubble of a blackish beard, then stepped briskly outside the tent flap.

The man climbing from the light and battered rig wore a threadbare frock coat. A hat the color of thoroughly used chewing tobacco was jammed on his furrowed brow. Older than Wilcox — fortyish — he advanced with a sprightly step and a sly scowl. Four husky Buffalo Soldiers converged and surrounded him, carbines held in front of massive blue-bloused chests.

"So, it's you!" exclaimed Jenks Wilcox.

"The bivouac can be seen plainly from town," Frock Coat barked. "I guessed it might be you, come back this way again." The voice had a menacing tone, but at the same time soft-pitched and smooth as sorghum. "Reckon I owe you something from your last time through. You remember, I'm sure."

Now Jenks Wilcox saw the padded leather case tucked high under the man's left arm. He wore no gun at his belt. The box caught and reflected the setting, pumpkin sun. "Let the visitor past, men," the officer ordered. Obediently the troopers fell back. "You and me, then, Doc. Just the two of us. Inside or out here?"

"Could run late with this. Fewer flies inside the tent, most likely." The hawk-lean features hadn't softened.

Jenks Wilcox looked under a strain, as well. He turned to the black man beside him. "Sergeant Meadow, we'll not be disturbed, I trust. The doctor and I have a grudge match."

"I understand, Captain." The man called 'doctor' stepped past the noncom and snapped open the case. The set of gleaming, ornate chessmen seemed to glow with magic power in the day's last rays. They were impressive specimens of the carver's art, pale ivory and ebony, inlaid with silver.

Jenks Wilcox relaxed his stern face and laughed. "I'll light the Argand lamp, Doctor Beauregard Lee of Perdition Springs. Then we'll begin play."

The Bear Claw Saloon was Perdition Springs' largest, which wasn't saying much. The single long and narrow room possessed a door at the front and a door at the back, and no windows. Along one wall, a bar of pine boards had been hammered together in such slipshod fashion that the patrons were forced to beware of splinters. The idea of paint had occurred to nobody. The pole beams that supported the roof held aloft spaced Rochester lamps.

The lamps' rays penetrated the swirling smoke haze in the place, but the light was dim and the wicks turned down low. A few paintings of nude females were obscured by shadows and smoke. Patrons stood along the bar, drinking diligently. Bottles clanked, drinkers whooped and talked, and there was the rattle of the wheel of fortune that dominated space near the bar. Two or three men stood around it, placing bets. A few additional gamblers sat at tables in the rear, laughing and slapping down their cards.

"Lordy, fellers, I guess I've died and went to heaven," Corporal Shadrach Jones allowed, gesturing to his companions. The noncom and five other Buffalo Soldiers stood inside the batwing swinging doors and peered about with the wide eyes of the newly arrived. Privates Cato Sweet and Theopholus McGee slapped Jones's back and sent their friend stumbling forward. They followed his lead toward the bar. Privates Jim Boze and Ben Abernathy brought up the rear.

The booted and dusty men in blue shoved back their campaign hats as they bellied against the panel, hoisted boots to the room's one luxurious touch, a dented and tarnished brass rail. When Jim Boze whooped out "Whiskey!" however, he was far from prepared for what happened next. Nothing.

At the end of the bar a henna-headed "soiled dove" strolled past wearing a knee-length dress of red. But she didn't look the Buffalo Soldiers' way. Neither did a prospector as he bawled for a refilled glass. Nor did the saloonkeeper himself, who waltzed by with gaze averted.

"Hey there, mister!" Private Sweet's throat was dry as fall cornshucks, but he could holler, and holler he did — loudly.

The wheel of fortune clanked and spun. Cards slapped down.

The bar dog fetched an unlabeled bottle to slam down in front of the prospector.

There was a bit of wrangling over the payment that the grizzled bearded man made in gold dust. The bar dog hadn't trimmed the thumbnail that he used to measure, and the quantity he demanded was over-large. Still, everyone up and down the bar stayed rowdily and drunkenly jovial.

All except the neglected Buffalo Soldiers.

Corporal Jones opined it was time to take a hand. He whacked his gauntlets on the bar. He kicked a zinc spittoon and set it to spinning. No one paid mind. Roughly attired muleskinners, stage-line hostlers, and miners laughed and talked, the whole while swilling fiery crackskull.

The several better-dressed townsmen — business owners — were as good at ignoring the Army presence as were the rest. One crew with particularly trail-grimed and ragged clothes did cast glances at Jones and Boze and the others. Their eyes were piggish and angry, under brows as threatening as winter thunderheads.

Shadrach Jones's sweaty dark face was blank as he again aimed his boot toe at the spittoon. This time the kick sent the bell-round thing over, and the contents, brown and slimy, slopped a bystander's pantleg and boot. The pantleg was torn and had been patched often, and the boot leather was sadly cracked, but a roar of outrage burst from the owner, a top-heavy freight-wagon bullwhacker. The man reached for the braided blacksnake coiled at his belt.

"Goddamn your hog-stupid, black nigger's soul! Now I got to whup your hog-stupid, black nigger's ass!"

With this the drover's hand streaked to the big whip's stock. Backing up, he managed to clear space around him. Scarlike lips peeled from rotten stumps of teeth, and the giant's arm drew back.

Private McGee didn't wait. The black soldier's big frame was as solid as the drover's, and he slammed Foul Teeth squarely in the chest with a lowered shoulder. The whip was wrenched from the white man's hammy hand.

"Hey!" another of the saloon's white patrons yelled.

"Can't no nigger go hittin' on no whites!"

"Not and get away with it!"

And then the loudest outcry of all surged through the room. "Only five o' the black-ass pony sojers, by God! Let's teach the sons of bitches a lesson!"

The saloon keeper himself let out a shout. "Yeah! One they won't forget!"

A giant in shotgun chaps wrenched the wheel of fortune from its axle. The houseman snatched a flung miniature magnet from the air and pocketed it. The wild-horse wrangler hurled the gaudy painted wheel at McGee and Boze. It shattered against their chests, flinging both men back.

Cato Sweet shouted: "We got to defend ourselves!"

"Do it!" were Corporal Jones's whooped words. He was rolling up his sleeves.

All up and down the bar and throughout the room, white hands clasped around bottles, billiard cues, or dice rakes. Chairs were smashed. Chair legs became clubs.

"Guess they tried to tell us we ain't welcome," McGee told Sweet.

The big black man snarled. "We're U. S. Cavalry, and we kill the Injuns and save the town. Ought to get treated like men, not low-down hounds!"

A white blacksmith smashed a fist to Jim Boze's ribs. A white typesetter threw a bottle at Theopholus McGee's head. Ben Abernathy reeled back at a white monte-thrower's kick to his groin.

"Lordy, they outnumber us two to one!"

"Rain Cloud's Arapahoes," whooped Corporal Jones. "Had us twenty to one, they did, up at Fort Remount in Dakota! And who won then?"

"Why, the Buffalo Soldiers did!"

And now the Buffalo Soldiers of E Company, Fort Bowie, waded into the battle of the Bear Claw Saloon.

Chapter Eleven

"Colonel Thornhill is indisposed again?" Shelby Frye inquired, as a freshly shaved and natty Marcus Cavanaugh walked into the orderly room and crossed the splash of morning sunlight that shone through the window. The chiseled, tanned face of the major turned to the adjutant and gave a curt nod. The captain, bucking for promotion, sat behind his desk, rigidly erect. He might as well have a poker up his rectum, Marcus thought, returning his salute.

He hung his kepi on its wall peg and took his own seat, rummaging purposefully in a drawer. He drew out a thin sheaf of papers filled with handwriting and spread them on the desktop.

"It's the third morning this week," Frye observed.

"I can count, Captain." Marcus' voice was crisp and cool. "So it happens that our commander sometimes sleeps through reveille. I've known generals who did the same. After thirty years of service to his country, it isn't as if Thornhill needed lessons in discipline."

The captain wore an oily, small smile. "Unless it's self-discipline."

Marcus had begun reading the sheet in front of him.

"I said — "

"I'm not going to defend our commander to you outright, Captain. It isn't as if you didn't know my feelings. The man is bereaved, he has only three months to serve before taking honorable retirement. He's been a fine officer throughout a career distinguished — "

"Don't you mean *un*-distinguished?"

"The man served on General Meade's staff in the War."

"And today Ulysses S. Grant is president, and Meade's left the military, thanks to his old rivals' animosity. One wishes that other excess baggage in this man's army — "

Marcus gave up and laid aside the paper. "I know you harbor a lot of bitterness, Captain," he said quietly. "You were brevetted a full colonel once upon a time for accomplishments in the War between the States. Were dropped back to captaincy with the coming of the peace, and given Washington duty polishing apples inside the War Department.

"How long have you been in the same rank now, Frye? Nine years? That's a hell of a trial, mister, I admit. But promotions come through campaign action in the Army these days. That you know as well as I, and'll have to live with it."

The tone of the executive officer's voice had silenced Shelby Frye. Although his ramrod posture hadn't slumped, his features had. The mouth was a bracketed slit.

"Captain," Marcus pursued, "I expect to hear no more hints disapproving of Colonel Thornhill. And you'll do well not to utter any more, even outside my earshot. Do I make myself clear?"

"You make yourself perfectly clear."

Marcus tried a light remark to cut the strain. "Doesn't the old saying go that nobody's perfect?"

Frye remained sour-faced. The joke failed to take hold.

After a few minutes of taut silence, the orderly thrust his kepi-clad head into the room. "Lieutenant Aaron Neel asking to see you, Major."

"Well I'm as available as I'll ever be, Sergeant Plover. Send him right on in."

"If you'll excuse me," Captain Frye grumbled, rising. "I have chores to do out around the post." In his kepi, with his burnished buttons winking, the adjutant marched through the headquarters front door as if on parade. But Marcus Cavanaugh wasn't by himself long enough to get lonely. A tall, slim slat of a man, Lieutenant Aaron Neel entered, and he brought someone with him.

The second man was a stocky Apache buck with a particularly ferocious cast to his bronze face. He wore the motley clothing of the typical army Indian scout working out of Fort Bowie: the calf-high moccasins that could be turned up to cover the knees; a pair of twill dungaree pants, over which hung the flapping breechcloth; a gingham shirt with a nondescript checked pattern; long, raven-black hair that hung thick to below the shoulders; and the red cloth headband.

Marcus Cavanaugh looked him up and down, his sharp gaze finally coming to rest on the heavy cartridge belt that cinched the redskin's waist. In one hand he carried a nine-shot Spencer carbine, older issue, but still a fine and deadly weapon. In his other arm, the Apache cradled a mysterious deerskin sack.

Marcus greeted the commander of the scout company. "Lieutenant Neel, what's up?" Neel saluted and made a quick introduction of his companion. "Major

Cavanaugh, this is Desalin. You recall, I'm sure, those settler's wagons that were found attacked weeks ago near Thunderhorse. After the massacre it was Lieutenant Claypoole's company that drew the assignment of trying to track and pursue the hostiles, even though the trail was several days old. Well, as it happened, the tracks did their petering out in the malpais lava beds below the foothills."

"I remember all that, Neel."

"Thank you, sir. Then I'll go on to tell the rest. The troopers that day came up dry in more ways than one. They ran low on water and had to turn back, and they failed to sight Nantaje's band of Chiricahuas. But when the Mescalero Apache scouts were called to rejoin the company, Desalin, here, had ranged far ahead of the rest. And he found something. The remains of a cold camp — and a captive the broncos had taken! A young white woman! She'd been buried to her neck beside an ant hill, and was near death. Most of her face had been eaten away, and what was left was a swollen, eyeless mess."

"Good God!"

"There's more. Desalin talked to the girl in English, and she was able to respond. To make the story short, she described a certain warrior from the band that killed her family and raped her. Here the amazing part starts! Desalin recognized the description! The deformed arm and the scarred face of the redskin she'd feared most — it had to be one of Desalin's own cousins! One he knew to have a squaw on the Seven Rivers reservation. The girl died before Desalin could free her, but our scout took it on himself to go straight to Seven Rivers. It was a matter of saving time, you see."

Marcus Cavanaugh's mind was racing. "Of course it would've been sensible, if not in strict accordance with standing orders. Desalin might've found his cousin at

Seven Rivers and been able to extract the exact location of Nantaje's hideout."

"That was the idea." Lieutenant Neel took a glance at the red man, then rushed on. "And Desalin did encounter his cousin Fights Wolf With Hands. The pair had a bloody donnybrook, the wild one being close-mouthed. And another kinsman joined the knife duel besides! Jesus!"

"Desalin returned here," Marcus said. "That means he must have killed his foes. Isn't that so?"

"It surely is, and he reported in to me just twenty minutes ago. With the trophies!"

"You mean — ?"

Desalin, his black eyes *zopilote* fierce and glittering, took a step toward the desk. Onto its top he smacked the deerskin sack, which made a slapping sound. Marcus Cavanaugh sucked in breath and readied himself. Copper-skinned hands loosed the drawstrings.

The scout shook the bag and out rolled two human heads. Indian heads, both with contorted expressions, for their owners had died in ghastly pain. Residual gore from the torn sinews of neck stumps drooled on the desk top. In the corner of the room near the door, the weak-stomached orderly gagged. Desalin grunted with pride.

"So he killed both the kinsmen who'd taken part in the raid." Marcus put words to what he'd guessed.

"One was his cousin," Aaron Neel announced, pointing. "The other over here, without the wolf-teeth scars, is Desalin's father."

Trumpeter Dud Gideon puckered up and blew "Boots and Saddles." The desert air on the outskirts of Perdition Springs rang with the stirring notes. Buffalo Soldiers scurried to their horses. At the urgings of First Sergeant Meadow, they stepped in leather and mounted.

Word had come in late morning from the posted scouts. The heavy wagons of munitions and supplies had crossed the ridge and were rolling across the flat. E Company was in the path of the many ponderous six-hitch mule teams. The bone-white bonnets of the Studebaker prairie schooners billowed and reflected glare. Private Henry Dobbs galloped up to the newly mounted column and threw a hurried salute to the first sergeant and the officer in command.

"Captain Wilcox, suh!"

"Spit out your news, Private."

"Lieutenant John Christiansen commanding D company from Fort Craig is in charge of the present escort, suh! He means to turn the train over to you, he's said, without the need of the drovers callin' a halt. He'll be ridin' over directly, suh! That's his message, suh!"

"Duly noted," said Jenks Wilcox. "And thank you, Private." The sweat-sheened brown face looked pleased. Wilcox turned to Meadow. "Sergeant, it's as I surmised. Do you make out the commander over there?"

Meadow held his field glasses to his eyes. He scanned the surrounding ridges, depressions, and flats. The total effect of the monotonous terrain was to create a desolate model of hell. The only movement was of the wagons, the teams, and the distant cavalry column, their horses plodding.

"That Captain Christiansen, he appears somethin' of a hopeful sort," the sergeant rasped. "In the middle of Injun country like he is, and he don't even have no flank guards out. Maybe he's another greenhorn."

Under the rakish folded hatbrim, Jenks Wilcox squinted. "Order four men out of the column to ride flank as soon as we take over, Sergeant. And that time won't be many minutes off. Oh, and I'll want an advance party — scouts — and a rear guard as well, just in case."

"Like up in Dakota, among the Sioux, Captain. It do be startin' to look like old times."

"Except for my feeling that the Apaches are even more dangerous than the Sioux, Meadow. And combined with this most devilish country, where we're aliens and the redskins are the ones at home — well, a man, black or white, can get damned uneasy." Wilcox mopped sweat. "By the way, make sure the flankers aren't of that bunch from the saloon brawl last night. I don't want to depend on eyes half-swelled shut and ears ringing from too many blows from fists."

"Still, we got to be proud of Jones and McGee and Sweet and Boze and Abernathy, sir! They've done this troop right proud."

Jenks Wilcox glanced at the head of the column, where the anointed battlers sat their mounts and nursed their aches. He shook his head in disapproval, but just the same couldn't completely suppress a grin. The captain knew what must have sparked the near riot he'd heard described. The whites-versus-blacks thing again. It had surfaced even down here where, by rights, townsmen should thank the soldiers — even Buffalo Soldiers — for the protection that kept them alive.

The lucky thing at the moment was that the four privates and the corporal had fought their way clear of trouble at the Bear Claw Saloon without suffering injury beyond a few scratches and scrapes. There had been no gun play or even knife play. And against more than a dozen of the angry hell-raisers who'd taken insult at having Buffalo Soldiers take a drink.

Yes, damned lucky.

Luckier than Jenks Wilcox had been up against his own adversary last night, Dr. Lee. The foxy medical man had again checkmated him after a long and well-played game of chess. The Southern doctor was a diabolical genius of the board.

As the teams and wagons drew slowly abreast the mounted black troopers of E Company, Wilcox spied a heavy-set officer and a stick-thin noncom peeling off from the escort column and coming toward him at a trot.

"Get set, Meadow," Wilcox breathed. "I'll have the troop moving out in a few minutes."

"I'm ready, suh. The men, they'll be just as ready."

Wilcox called in friendly fashion to the fatigued blond officer whose escort his own company would soon replace.

"Lieutenant Christiansen, I believe? Welcome to Arizona Territory!"

As the officers exchanged salutes off beside the road, the Buffalo Soldiers waited and watched. Ben Abernathy nearly choked on wheel dust as wagon after wagon rolled by. He breathed through puffy lips that had been impacted by a chairleg in last night's fracas. Now he owned the granddaddy of all headaches, and he hadn't even managed to take one drink. "I reckon I've gone to hell," he groaned.

"'Reckon?' Pshaw, Ben, m'boy!" Cato Sweet rasped through broken and loose front teeth. "I do know I'm there! My bruises, they say it for damn sure!"

The two Apaches viewed the passing column from behind mesquite clumps on the distant ridge, shielding eyes with cupped hands against the shimmering glare. Their savage faces were scowling. Bands of war paint were sketched across their cheekbones and the bridges of their noses. Both were well armed from thieving forays across the border in Sonora. They clutched Winchester Model 73's, which they'd liberally greased with animal fat.

Behind the leader and his companion, in one of the ravines that laced the terrain's backbone, two dozen warriors, in full battle array of cartridge belts and paint, waited. Some held lances, clubs, bows, and arrows, the traditional Apache tools of combat. Most handled repeating rifles and squirmed impatiently.

A warrior with a crooked nose asked his war leader, "Now we ride down and kill them all, and take the guns and goods?"

Nantaje scowled, but made no move. "Not now," he said. "But soon, my brother. Very soon."

Chapter Twelve

Major Marcus Cavanaugh strode along a familiar foot-path inside the tall, protective walls of Fort Bowie. It led among the closely spaced houses assigned to those officers who were married or had families. The route was a shortcut from the ordnance and commissary storehouses where he'd been making inspections. He'd noticed a few lapses in regulations, and given corrective orders. Now, on his way back to headquarters by way of Colonel Thornhill's, he stepped out briskly. It was his wish to catch the commander at his house before noon.

The day was another scorcher, and the post was far from bustling. The fatigue details shuffled listlessly at their tedious painting and cleaning chores. In the paddock, horses stood with drooping heads. Laundresses on soapsuds row sweated over their tubs. Shovelers in the stables invented new curses. Marcus feared for the sentries' attention while on lookout. He'd ordered today's sergeants of the guard to keep their own eyes peeled.

And now emerging from the dwelling just ahead was a dark-haired vision in a frilly gingham frock. No matter what the weather, summer's heat or winter's cold, Sophia Frye always managed to look her best. Since her delicate features and comely figure made her quite a handsome woman, her best was very fine indeed. She leaned over the porch rail and waved her pocket handkerchief at Marcus.

"Oh, Major Cavanaugh! How good to see you!"

He touched the brim of his kepi gallantly, and half bowed to her. "Sophia. And how are you this morning?"

For the moment they were alone together in this particular corner of the post. No one passed on the path. The sun beat straight down, nearly overpowering the couple. "Won't you stop a minute in the porch's shade?"

"Well, I suppose just a minute, not much more, won't hurt."

"I'd like a word or two with you, Marcus."

"Somehow I'd guessed."

Face to face now with the wife of the adjutant, Marcus started to feel uncomfortable. She'd approached him more than once before with her vaguely discontented air. She seemed to feel she might have married beneath her station. Marcus had decided that she'd better start making the best of things. The lot of the officer's woman on a rough frontier post could be monotonous at best, miserable at worst. But Marcus had met some very happy females engrossed in loving their husbands, no matter what. Sophia Frye wasn't one of these. He wondered idly what she'd have to say this time.

"Marcus, it's about Shelby. The man's plain sour. You may have guessed the kind of man he is."

Marcus had.

"But it's not entirely his fault. His career has been blighted. He rocketed to the rank of full colonel rather early, and then — "

Marcus spoke carefully to the woman. "Many soldiers have lost brevet rankings that they once held, Sophia. A sergeant major that I knew up at Fort Lincoln had been a brigadier. The likes of Gettysburg created a host of promotions. One has to be a man about these things, and stand up to disappointment. If your husband can't do that — "

"It would mean so much to him — and me — if he could be promoted again. He knows the way, actually. It's distinction in battle. But he seems caught in the middle, down here at Bowie. Adjutants merely perform paper work. Shelby needs the chance to get out from behind his desk."

"And into the field? On scouts?" Marcus tried to be persuasive. "By this time Shelby Frye's an older man. Oh, not doddering, but the years do add up. And so much of his career was spent in Washington. Now, the long rides in this intolerable heat against Apache foes, well, the strain can be intolerable. Don't you remember Lieutenant LeMay?

"Clay LeMay was a very green young officer. His foolishness nearly wiped out his company. He felt disgraced, and shot himself.

"Shelby Frye is older, but in many ways green, too. The warfare today in Arizona isn't like that in the conflict between North and South. No artillery barrages. Armies of infantry don't stand still and fire massed volleys. We're hit lightninglike by savages who strike and run. And with defeat comes death, either quickly or slowly. The Apaches show no mercy and take no bluecoat prisoners."

She looked perplexed. "But if my husband could only become happier — "

"He'd not make you unhappy?"

Sophia Frye went so far as to touch Marcus's sleeve. "Won't you speak to the colonel?"

"Sophia, it's my decision, just as much as Thornhill's. Captain Frye is a satisfactory desk soldier. In the field, who knows?"

"Is this your last word on the matter, Marcus Cavanaugh?"

"Yes."

There was a frown hovering on her face. It was much more than a pout. "Then I guess I have a decision to make." She pursed her lips tightly. "But that's my own business and none of yours! I'll bid good day to you, then, Major." She spun quickly on a trim heel and hurried inside.

A booming baritone erupted behind Marcus, and he turned to greet the approaching figure of the commander.

"Colonel Thornhill," Marcus greeted him. "I was just looking for you, sir." The casual, friendly salute was returned in kind.

"Spit it out then, Major. We'll talk on the way to officers' mess."

"About that letter that the dispatch rider brought. I've done some thinking — "

"You mean the one from San Francisco, of course. Hiram Titus's message. I, too, have been considering, Cavanaugh. He declares that he'll soon be starting on his way back here. Now, letters travel slowly in the West, and he could have overtaken his communication, or nearly so. He and the railroad friend Pearson could arrive in a few days."

"Or tomorrow."

"Or this afternoon. So it's up to us to be prepared. General Grummond of Division Headquarters wants the Apache problem licked. Titus will likely be the bearer of that word."

The colonel and the major were striding rapidly past the hospital. Marcus waved to the post surgeon, Major Cuppenwaldo. "With accompanying threats?" Marcus asked Thornhill.

"I have no doubt."

"We're doing all we can without additional men."

"We were sent those Buffalo Soldiers, I'm sure you recall. Major, we might consider mounting a campaign against Nantaje's force. Wipe out their remote strongholds in the mountains and badlands. The wily savage will never attend a parley. This Sentagolatha woman hasn't convinced him to."

"I don't know if she was able to get word to him. I haven't heard from her."

The colonel spoke firmly. "Learn if the message was ever delivered. And whether there's a possibility she might act for us as guide." Marcus Cavanaugh winced, then returned the salute of Private Kraus who was passing by. The major turned back to the colonel. "We have Lieutenant Neel's Mescaleros to do our scouting."

"Perhaps an alienated Chiricahua woman would know the Chiricahua strongholds best. We shouldn't, Major, take a risk of slips."

Marcus shook his head. "A decisive campaign in those damned badlands in front of Thunderhorse. It's Nantaje's own home ground, where his warriors know every pine grove, every barranca. And we thought that Clayton LeMay was so foolish to commit suicide. But rest assured, Colonel, I will be working out those strategies."

They were at the officers' dining hall now, and about to enter the low, rambling structure. Before they could do so, however, Thornhill fixed Marcus with an earnest stare. "The most important thing for us, Cavanaugh, in the days and weeks ahead, is that the Fort Bowie regiment must suffer no disasters, no costly defeats. Hope for that!"

Marcus Cavanaugh nodded.

Inside the building at a window, Shelby Frye was watching, his face a mask. Only the captain's eyes registered emotion. These were hard and cold as pebbles from a mountain stream.

"You do well, my brother," the broken-nosed Chiricahua told Nantaje across the distance that separated their standing ponies. Mongash and the raid leader sat on their animals below the lip of the sand-crusted ridge. Behind them and downslope, the massed band of more than twenty-five warriors waited, lances, bows and arrows, rifles at the ready. They only awaited their leader's signal by war cry to mount and ride to action.

They were confident that their medicine was good. The night before there had been strong dancing around flickering campfires.

For most of the night the bright stars had shone down on the posturing, stamping bronco bucks. They'd grimaced fiercely while they leaped and ran in place, chanting their monotonous *hay-nay-nays*. Prayers were sung over weapons, and even the lightning god had been asked for his aid. The warriors had taken to their ponies' backs at first dawn's blush, eager to spill the thin, weak blood of the rabbit-timid White Eyes.

It was the morning of the second day. The procession of bonneted wagons had toiled off slowly toward the far stronghold fort of the White Eyes. With it had rolled the cargo of army supplies. But, although ammunition was a precious commodity to renegades, Nantaje was no fool.

The escorting bluecoats from the north had watered their horses, rested for a while, then ridden back along the same wagon trace down which they'd come. That company of troops had been replaced with the Fort Bowie contingent. In it were no more fighting men than Nantaje had. But Nantaje, coyote-sly, did not wish to pay for victory with many warriors' lives. The escort were the bluecoats with the black skins, the ones called the Buffalo Soldiers. To the People, the buffalo was sacred. The men with hair like the sacred creature could be invested with its power.

Now all the bluecoats had gone far from the ugly White Eyes blot on the desert, Perdition Springs. With them had gone the town's real protection. The town's only defense was in the hands and weapons of a few men.

"You do well, my brother." Nantaje scratched a White Eyes sulfur match, dropping the tiny flame on a carefully laid pile of tinder. The mesquite branches, dried bone-brittle by the furnace winds, glowed red, then flamed and smoked. Soon a cone-shaped flood of black smoke spired toward the sky.

Nantaje swiftly stripped to the waist. The other warriors also stripped and leaped on their ponies' backs. "Now the White Eyes come," Nantaje grunted. And this was true. Mounted men from town were now spurring hell for leather across the caliche flats. They supposed that there'd been trouble for some settler with a wagon. Women and and children might be in danger. Maybe a small band of Ariraipas had jumped the reservation.

On the far side of town, a lone warrior who'd been sent to find the telegraph line scurried up the peeled-log pole. He slashed the wire through and descended hastily, then leaped to his mount's back and urged the pony to a gallop.

The white men rode to the imagined rescue brandishing six-guns and carbines. There was the saloonkeeper with a stubby sawed-off Piedmont fowling piece. And the son of an old trapper who'd appropriated his pap's cannonlike Sharps .50. Perdition Springs' menfolk strung out across the desert in a hard-spurring mob. There were twenty horsemen in the bunch from town. Some of them were drunk. Some of the rest were youths in their teens.

They stormed down arroyos and over the low hilltops, their horses' hooves scattering dust and gravel in the headlong run. Below the ridge, Nantaje gestured with a sinewy bronze arm. His new Winchester flashed in a swift arc. " *Uga-she*," he shouted. "Forward!"

His warriors spread in a long line abreast, imitative of the cavalry. They kneed their ponies' flanks and the animals sprang forward. The band hurtled up the slope and over the top of the ridge, a whooping, shrieking, savage avalanche, tearing down on the surprised men of Perdition Springs.

"Kill! Kill! *Kill*!" was the redskins' resounding cry. Gunfire burst in a staccato of rattling sound and blooming puffs of smoke. There was panic among the townsmen, and notions of counterattack were swallowed in tides of shock and fear.

"Jesus Christ in a handcart, fellers! Let's hightail!"

The white men's mounts strove their mightiest, but the trap that had been so well laid was now effectively sprung. Whites and the horses of whites fell on all sides, dropped by bullets and arrows that flew as thick as a winter hailstorm. The Apache band fanned wide, circling as they fired, cutting off retreat. Blood-lust seethed in the Indians' vengeful brains. The impact of bullets sent more townsmen catapulting from saddles. One flipped in spectacular somersault as he died. Another's head burst apart from a 200-grain slug.

"Kill! Kill! Kill!" shrieked the crazed Apache raiders.

The mayor of Perdition Springs was violently driven from the saddle, shot through the head. His brother-in-law, the blacksmith, was speared by a nine-foot war lance. He kept his mount for a few galloping yards, until his intestines spilled from his horribly ripped gut.

"Where are the goddamn pony soldiers?" Asa Dunbridge hollered.

"Nowhere to be seen!" screeched Jake McCoy, professional monte thrower. As he whooped, he tossed a six-gun shot, and saw an Apache bronco pitch headfirst to the dirt. But then the gambler's luck turned, when an arrow with an iron tip punched him in the back. Agony centered at the wound and flowed outward. Jake's knees parted from the running roan's flanks, and the howling man toppled sideways.

"Christ, Jake, your stirrup!" McCoy's ankle was hung up, and he was dragged. His bobbing head struck a rock and burst.

"Kill!" Nantaje whooped. From the running dun he aimed his Winchester at yet another White Eyes, triggered, and the man went down. The rifle's barrel was hot in his big bronze hand. Still, he kept firing without pause. He killed a rider in a wide sombrero. He killed the rider's pinto horse.

Glancing first to the right, then the left, the raider chief took in the havoc and grinned wickedly. Almost all the White Eyes that had ridden from the town were dead. Directly ahead of the dun pony, one was left afoot, however. Nantaje veered his mount that way. He rode down the frantically fleeing towhead youth. The pony's hoofs hammered the yielding body, crushing bones, muscle, and organs.

"Ya-eee-*ee*!" the kid screamed.

Nantaje rode on. Only a few Chiricahua warriors were dead or had so much as sustained wounds. Across the battleground, strewn with slain White Eyes, kill-crazed eyes sought the next signal of the war leader.

Nantaje shouted hate and rage, and wheeled his horse toward the pitiful small town itself. "Kill!"

"Kill! Kill! Kill!" The yipping cry was taken up.

The Apache raiders thundered into Perdition Springs like devils straight from hell.

Chapter Thirteen

As Nantaje's marauders charged up the narrow single street of Perdition Springs, they drove the females, the children, and the old-timers before them like so many scared sheep. Arrows brought down some, bullets others. Nantaje rode in the forefront of the raid, wielding a war club of heavy lightning-split mountain oak.

He batted a woman who'd frozen in fright. She staggered into a water trough, her once-lovely face mushed to crimson jelly. An ancient grandfather stopped in his tracks, spun, and brought up a rusty dragoon pistol. Mongash, the broken-nosed warrior, darted in on his pony to knock the graybeard careening. The shot he fired in his death throes only ventilated air.

Another female ran full-tilt with hoisted skirts. Some townsfolk had fled into buildings. She was struggling to follow them. She was killed by a bullet from one of the saloon's defenders, got off in haste. She flopped across a sprawled boy, her blood and brain matter splashing over him. Arrows stuck from the youngster's torso and from his neck. His death had been merciful, over in an instant, unlike what was so painfully in store for the unlucky ones.

In the tiny cabin that was the telegraph office, Jud Coogan had been trying to work his silent, useless key. Finally he grunted a virulent "Goddamn!" and hurled his eyeshade aside. He lurched from his chair and over to the window, in time to have it shatter in his face, dissolving in a sleet storm of flying glass. His features turned red from rivering blood. Blinded, he groped and stumbled to the slippery, shard-strewn floor.

In the Bear Claw Saloon, whores and respectable women clutched the few guns that they'd somehow managed to assemble. Most of the town's weapons had traveled with its men, and were now in Apache hands. Nell Albright had taken command. Before she'd become middle-aged and jaded, she'd been a pretty strong gal. She'd pioneered the gold-rush towns, seen bloodshed, and contributed her quota. Now the plowshare-handle of a six-pound Walker Colt filled her palm. She could hardly hold the huge old six-gun level.

"That scattergun loaded?" Nell queried Henrietta Van Dorsten, the preacher's daughter. Reverend Van Dorsten himself sprawled dead in the street outside. The young woman was quaking in her grief and shock.

"It's loaded." Henrietta Van Dorsten's cheeks were wet with tears.

"The Spencer carbine?"

"Cocked and trigger ready!" Julia Harkness of Harkness's Mercantile paid no mind to her smudged dress and thoroughly mussed blond hair.

Busty Mamie Overhauser peeped over the upturned table that blocked the batwings. "Christ, here they come," the whore breathed.

"Where?"

"Look out behind us!"

Henrietta and Nell spun together, their long full-cut skirts billowing. Mamie fired her quail gun. The Apache coming through the rear doorwell yelled. The hooting redskins were piling in, launching arrows from powerfully strung elm-wood bows. Nell took a missile in the shoulder. A sharp flint arrowhead drove completely through the Harkness woman's thigh. Almost immediately all the females were disarmed and subdued. In another minute their dresses were yanked away, and they were shoved to the floor, naked and screeching.

Then their real troubles began.

There was more resistance in the town than Nantaje had anticipated. Up and down the dusty street, through shut-up buildings' windows, guns of all descriptions and calibers thrust, raining hurt on Apache raiders who'd blundered into range. The war leader rode down a last victim, a girl-child, splitting her skull with a blow of his club that left the weapon red and glistening. Then he kneed the dun pony in among the warriors grouped by the livery corral. Within the earth-brick confines, panicky mules brayed and horses lashed out, kicking. Still, a few Apaches labored to contain the bunch, which was worth the effort to steal.

"Ho!" cried Mongash, from his spotted pony's plunging back.

"Ho!"

Nantaje sent warriors into the low hay barn, and they emerged twisting wads of flammable fodder, passing them to the riders. With an eager yipping chorus, the bucks wheeled and charged back up the street, striking lucifers, igniting their torches. Ignoring the gunfire from the defended dwellings, the savage raiders rode, swept fast and furiously near, drew back sinewy arms and hurled flame. Smoke belched from the straw roofs, sparks erupted skyward in colorful orange bursts.

"Kill! Kill! Kill!" The frenzied death call was renewed. Hungry flames roared upward, the bright orange glow reflecting from the pall of smoke. Within the buildings, heat and pressure built. Men's and women's lungs were seared by the venomous hot fumes. The blazing ceiling of the Red Garter Saloon collapsed, setting afire the few defenders there. They died screaming.

From the superheated walls of Doc Lee's office, Lee and another man burst, methodically triggering six-guns. The pard winged a bronco who rode past. The doc shot a horse dead, and it went down in a thrashing heap. Then the partner's heart took a bullet, as did the medical man's left foot.

"Jesus, I'm wounded!" He lay on his back and looked up at the dark smoke-filled sky. All the surrounding area was filled with crackling flames, and the shouts of people in pain made shrill cacophony. Dr. Beauregard Lee tried to point the barrel of his Smith & Wesson to his graying temple. The weapon was kicked away.

An Apache dropped beside him, leering. A second rattled off some guttural words. Now the doctor realized his present hurt was slight. That what was to come would be far worse. Lee could understand a smattering of the Chiricahua tongue. Nantaje had decreed that the wounded man be stripped for torture. The warriors were eager to comply.

It was another quiet and monotonous afternoon at Fort Bowie. The brutal sun hammered down as usual, and the sifting dust raised by horses in the mounted drill provided the usual saffron haze. Marcus Cavanaugh sat at his desk in the headquarters building and kept from sneezing through sheer willpower. Willpower helped the major with his work, as well.

He had diminished the pile of papers on the left side of the desk by shuffling them to the right side. Most were requests for transfer from various officers, which he'd regretfully found impossible to oblige. They were shorthanded in the officer department at Bowie, just as they were with enlisted troopers. At the moment most of the men were out on the patrols that had been stepped-up.

The more they went looking for bronco Apaches, the fewer they found. The Indians had the uncanny skill to melt into the wild desert country like ghosts. They appeared when they wanted to, wrought their havoc, and then vanished again. But they were out there somewhere. The remains of the hell they raised kept always turning up. And it was always gruesome beyond one's ghastliest nightmares.

The major cast his glance over at Colonel Thornhill, busy at his own desk. The post commander's eyes were bloodshot and bagged, his square face deeply seamed. He was showing his years more with each passing, wearing day, and Marcus knew the nights were equally tough on the aging officer, spent as they inevitably were with solace from a bottle. In a way, Marcus was contemptuous of a man who did what the colonel was doing — destroying himself. But in another way he had some understanding.

He'd known Mrs. Thornhill briefly before she'd been carried off by sudden illness, and she was both beautiful and charming, younger than her husband by a dozen years. One could see why the colonel, missing Becky, had lost his old passions for army interests.

Marcus Cavanaugh shifted in his seat, scrubbed his chin with a blue flannel sleeve. If he could see Thornhill through the next few months, the man could retire in honor to Wisconsin and live with his grown daughter and her family. She and her husband had three young kids. Marcus's hunch was that the grandchildren would spark new meaning in Frank Thornhill's life.

Thornhill coughed softly, tossing down his pen.

"Something the matter, Colonel?"

"I see the orderly through the window there, and he's hotfooting it across the quadrangle. Something's up, all right."

Both the officers were on their feet when Sergeant Plover charged through the door.

"Colonel! Major!" The noncom threw a quick salute, but didn't wait for the returns. "The post's telegraph operator says to notify you that he's not getting messages through on the north line up New Mexico way. He can't even raise Perdition Springs, so he's guessing the wire's down between here and the town. Likely cut by the Apaches. Could it be they've attacked the little place?"

"Where Nantaje is concerned," Marcus said, "it's more than merely possible. It's damned likely. Good God, the supply train's up in that area, too! Could Wilcox and his E Company have been jumped?"

Thornhill's vacant look had turned more focused. Thoughts were percolating in his brain, as in the major's.

"I don't think so, sir!" Plover said.

Both the officers' eyes flew to the orderly. "I say it, sir, because, as it happens, there's more to tell. The sentries on the parapets have just now spotted a column of troops and a large train of wagons on the road from up north. They should be rolling into Bowie within the hour, Colonel. I have no doubt that it's Company E because the lookouts' binoculars picked out the troopers' dark skins. Oh, and there's a sprung ambulance and its team in the incoming party, too."

"I can guess what that means."

"Hiram Titus of the Interior Department, returned!"

Marcus was in motion, jamming on his kepi and stalking toward the door. "Everything seems to be happening at once. We'll be sending a relief column to Perdition Springs, though God knows if reinforcements can be gotten there in time. The townsfolk may all be dead."

"If there's been a massacre — " Frank Thornhill wondered.

Marcus Cavanaugh paused. "If there has, General Grummond in San Francisco won't like it. Hiram Titus won't like it. And Colonel, you well know, I don't like Nantaje's boldness in these guerrilla strikes. That's why we're going to deal with the Apache question. Colonel, I want permission to take to the field myself! A flying column — two companies — ought to be able to move fast enough. And I've had my eye on those rough-and-ready Buffalo Soldiers!"

"E Company combined with another company? What if the renegades can't be tracked or caught up with? What if they simply melt into the desert, as they always have before?"

"If we don't catch Nantaje, at least it won't be for lack of trying. But first we'll head straight for Perdition Springs. What do you say, Colonel?"

There was a long and strained pause on Frank Thornhill's part. Finally he said, "After all due consideration, Major, I'm going to deny your request. For one thing, most of our companies are already off on patrols. The troopers left here are barely enough to defend the fort. For another thing, you're needed just now for more important matters. Titus and his railroad-man traveling companion have to be handled. The overall Apache question needs new strategies. It's a damned hectic time."

Marcus Cavanaugh's jaw dropped, and he went rigid in his stance. "But the situation at Perdition Springs — ?"

"Captain Wilcox can take his troop straight on back there. I say, start this evening, and perform a forced cavalry march clear through the night. Those Buffalo Soldiers won't have much chance to rest, but they'll have some — and of course they'll be provided with strong, fresh horses. That's simply all we can do with our limited manpower."

Marcus' shoulders didn't slump, but the expression on his face did. When he mouthed, "Yes, sir, Colonel," it was without enthusiasm.

Thornhill turned to Sergeant Plover. "Get Sergeant Major Brody over here. Have the trumpeter blow 'Assembly Call.' All this needs announcing to the post."

"Yessir!"

"Now, Major Cavanaugh, let's get ready to greet our civilian visitors one more time."

Duty remained duty, and Marcus was used to carrying out orders, even when his own notions ran contrary. But the tall major cursed. Wilcox would have the chance to see action, while he was more valuable back here at the post, stuck strategizing when the bullets were flying. He swallowed his complaint in silence, because duty was duty.

Outdoors the first silvery notes of the bugle were bouncing off the stockade walls. Marcus tugged his blouse and straightened his kepi. Then he strode with the colonel onto the veranda to watch the parade of arriving supply wagons.

It was well past the fleeting time of desert dusk, and the lamp in the post commander's office burned brightly. Marcus Cavanaugh had taken a chair at the end of the desk on Frank Thornhill's left, while Hiram Titus and Moody Pearson sat directly opposite the colonel. By this time everybody looked extremely tired. The discussion had been far-ranging, and had gone on for hours.

"Well," the slack-faced colonel was saying, his palms pressed to the desk top and his eyes flashing, "I guess we understand each other's views, at least, after all this. Even though we're far from agreeing with each other."

Hiram Titus wore an expression as smooth as the pressed suit he'd changed to in his quarters. Precious minutes had been lost while he'd freshened up after his journey, but he was a government high-up, felt entitled to such privileges, and so took them. Pearson, the railroad representative, had also washed himself and shaved. Marcus had never seen the oily fop other than immaculately groomed and in clothes of the finest broadcloth. He had an irritating little voice. At least today the fellow had let Titus do most of the talking.

"No, Colonel," Titus intoned resonantly, "There's no question but that we don't see eye-to-eye. You appear content with the way things are going here in the Department of Arizona. Seem to advocate more of the same with regard to Indian campaigns. Believe this land can do without railroads while the settlers' inrush lags. On every one of those points, yes, I find myself opposed."

Thornhill glanced at Marcus, and the tall major rolled his eyes upward in disgust. Thornhill cleared his throat. "You exaggerate, Mr. Titus. I've no interest in seeing this land go undeveloped. But I do have many years' experience dealing with Apaches. Their traditional way is to roam freely over all Apacheria. Crowd those Indians together in one tight hellhole, and you're asking for a rampage."

"I don't agree," Hiram Titus said. "Neither does General Grummond, or the Secretary of the Interior, or the Secretary of War. The directives I turned over to you today state it clearly. To make way for the building of the railroad, we must take back certain reservation lands."

"The ones comprising the better hunting grounds. The more suitable farm sites," Marcus thrust in harshly.

"Coincidentally, so it turns out. Does Mr. Pearson need to explain things further?"

"All he has there are maps, elevation figures, distance charts. Construction engineers' rigmarole!"

Pearson, who'd suddenly perked up, again subsided and pursed his lips.

There was a throb of trotting hoofbeats through the window. Colonel Thornhill raised his voice in order to be heard. "Instructions from my superiors, I'm forced to obey them, gentlemen." His face had gone glum. "Word will be got out to the peaceful chiefs on reservations of the government's new stand."

"As soon as possible!" The words had burst from Moody Pearson's smug mouth.

"Yes, as soon as possible." Hiram Titus's chins were quaking.

Thornhill turned to Marcus. "Major Cavanaugh, you've established good relations with Chief Gleheehaco. We may as well get this thing done. E Company marches tonight for Perdition Springs. The agency isn't far beyond. You will accompany Captain Wilcox's troopers. Hostiles might make it hot for a lone rider. When you reach the agency, you're to convey the message from the 'Great White Chief.' Tell Gleheehaco that his people must be crowded up again. We'll be hoping that he takes it well."

"Me? Ride with Captain Wilcox? I'll need to rush, sir!"

"The civilians will excuse you, I'm sure."

Marcus Cavanaugh rose, saluted, and strode for the door. In the doorway he turned. "Thank you, Colonel!"

In another second he was double-timing the shadowed path toward his quarters. He wouldn't be taking much, but among those few things, he wanted weapons.

Chapter Fourteen

"Mother of God!" Captain Jenks Wilcox hissed. The tanned, mussed, large-nosed man in command of E Company sat his mount beside Marcus Cavanaugh outside Perdition Springs. The sky was dotted with low-diving *zopilote* buzzards, and the focus of the great, ugly scavenger birds was the devastated town. The files of black troopers behind the officers felt their nostrils wrinkle. The stench was abominable.

The column had approached from downwind, and from the odors drifting far across the desert flat, fears of the worst had been growing for hours. On this second afternoon out from of Bowie, the men were sweat-sheened, bone-thirsty, and tired. Their commander had forced a rapid pace, well over the regulation twenty-five miles per twenty-four hours laid down by Upton's manual. In spite of their haste, as was now clear to eyes as well as noses, they were too late. The likelihood was, they'd been too late when they left the fort.

The broken telegraph wire somewhere out in the open stretches must surely have accompanied the

Apaches' opening charge. Why the townsfolk hadn't been able to retreat to buildings and repel or wait out Nantaje's fury, no living person could now know. Unless by a miracle they'd find a survivor to tell the story. But no horse soldier believed that they would.

"The redskins are long gone, Captain," Marcus stated. "Our own Mescalero scouts confirm it, so it ought to be safe for us to ride on in." He signaled with his arm. "Forward, ri-ide!"

With a creaking of saddles and a jingling of bit chains, the column began the last quarter mile of the Perdition Springs trek. Not one of the cavalrymen liked what he was being compelled to do at this place of death.

"Keep the horses from the troughs by the wells," Marcus ordered. "The water may be poisoned. We'll rely on the hogsheads our pack mules carry. Pass the word on."

"Yes, suh," snapped First Sergeant Meadow, and he shouted back over his shoulder to the riders coming up behind. His voice cracked from his own gullet-shrinking thirst.

Jenks Wilcox swiped at his perspiring, flaming cheeks, and his blouse sleeve came away wet. "Looks like a damned butcher's yard." Entering the town's sole street, he'd already glimpsed some bodies, although as yet only a comparative few. The scavenger birds had ravaged and torn them horribly with their long curved beaks. The *zopilotes* waddled and flopped among the dead people, dragging trails in the dusty earth with enormous funereal wings. Slimy entrails hung from raw-looking red heads. Beadlike eyes glared. At the men's approach, the birds scuttled off reluctantly. Most took ponderous, flapping flight.

"We'd best dismount and comb the place, captain," Marcus suggested bitterly. It was at times like this that he wished he smoked tobacco. He knew the junior officer sometimes did. "You and the men might as well light up your cigars," the major added. "I never saw a black man look green, but quite a few of them are starting to do so this day."

"Pee-*yew*!" The smell was sickening, disgustingly putrid, and overpowering. At least two days of broiling sun and heat had worked to rot the flesh the scavengers hadn't devoured, and the remains were hideously bloated and empurpled.

"Jesus, that one over there moved!" burst out a trooper. Some men who'd dismounted crawfished backward in understandable alarm.

"Shucks, that's just a blast o' nasty rotten gas!"

"The men seem to feel it," Jenks Wilcox murmured. "Goddamn, I'm starting to feel it, too."

"The restless spirits of the dead?" Marcus scoffed. "Get a grip on yourself, man. You'll need to if you're going to get through this afternoon. The worst is yet to be found, I'm betting. There's a curve up ahead in this miserable street. Prepare yourself."

As they continued to advance on foot, the next corpses that they encountered were still more shocking. Those passed back near the edge of town seemed to have died running for a safety they'd never gained. Now Marcus and Wilcox saw the remains of torture victims, those whose fate it had been to die slowly, and in unendurable agony. There were bodies of both sexes strewn about, but as often as not, the men couldn't be distinguished from the women. The softer body parts had been mutilated by broncos or ripped away by buzzards — or both.

There had been wholesale castrations, decapitations, and the skinning of helpless victims alive.

Some corpses were charred from fire, some carved by knives. A good many people had been staked down at

131

the wrists and ankles, spreadeagled while the barbaric torturers did their fiendish work. The corpses were caked with blackened, dried blood. Some lay pierced by dozens of arrows, presumably shot, one by one, into nonvital parts. That way the unfortunates had been kept alive to writhe and scream — and provide entertainment. But other methods, too, had been found amusing. Fires had been built in the vees of victim's crotches. Women's breasts and the males' members had been brutally hacked. Abdomens had been slashed and innards pulled out. The women would have been repeatedly raped. The act was typical of Apache raids.

Private Joe Cotten had seen a lot in his ten-year army career, but he found himself leaning on a charred hitchrail by a store, puking up his dinner. Corporal Shadrach Jones muffled his mouth with a bandanna against the smell. Through the wad of cloth he told Ben Abernathy, "Damn! This is worse'n my baddest dreams!"

Private Theopholus McGee kicked open the door to the Bear Claw, glanced inside, viewed smashed furniture, broken mirrors, and crockery. The room had been the scene of the brawl — townsmen versus Buffalo Soldiers.

"Didn't no white folks deserve this! They was bad, but they didn't deserve this!"

Private Cato Sweet was at McGee's elbow. "There's that big-mouth barkeeper, over there. Arms and legs and head lopped off."

"How you know him, Cato?"

"You remember. I punched his ear so it'd swell big. All that's left of the feller's face is that one swelled ear."

Outside, Marcus Cavanaugh shouted, "Sergeant Meadow! Form up burial details. There must be spades in some of these buildings. Or the men can use their own camp spades. If the town has no cemetery, create one."

"Yes, suh," Labe Meadow said.

Jenks Wilcox rode ahead of the major and the troopers. His gaze swept the remains of the slaughter, seeking, ever seeking. Smoke from the foul, cheap stogie stung both eyes and his overgrown, over-sensitive nose. The tobacco fumes were strong and acrid, but for once he was grateful he'd saved money on his brand.

Then, in the open space between blacksmith's and barber's shops, he caught sight of the mangled naked corpse of what had been a man. A man he recognized. Dr. Beauregard Lee had died exceptionally hard. He was staked to the ground like so many of those slain in Perdition Wells, but the tormentor here had possessed an appalling sense of butchery. Lee's eyelids had been stretched open and pinned that way by *cholla* spines, and his graying distinguished head wedged to face the sun. His mouth had been pried open and filled with sand. Many splinters of wood had been soaked in coal oil and driven into his legs, arms, trunk. Most, but not quite all, had then been ignited to sear the skin — and penetrate suffering flesh.

The medical man's genitals were missing from the body, leaving a cavity filled with hardened gore. Dr. Lee's face was frozen in a rigid, thoroughly revolting mask, reflective of all the man's last soul-shattering agony.

Marcus Cavanaugh came upon Wilcox and took note of the captain's shock. There was something personal about this particular one, the major surmised.

Jenks Wilcox turned to his superior, the squinting eyes lit by an angry fire. "Major Cavanaugh, this man was my friend. I just met him last month, only spent a few hours sitting at chess with him. He was a practitioner of the healing arts, and from what he told me, a dedicated one."

"The good ones and the evil ones, the Chiricahua raiders kill all the whites they can. That's why we're out here in this purgatory called San Simon Basin, Captain. Nobody told you a soldier's life was much other than hell."

Wilcox sucked his stogie till the end glowed red. "Nantaje's band, wasn't it?"

Marcus bobbed an assured nod. "Had to have been, by the number of warriors this slaughter took. He's the only war leader who's presently operating this big. And yet, he wouldn't try his hand against your company, not even to get Fort Bowie's supply train."

"You believe he knew — ?"

Marcus shrugged. "The Apaches know everything that goes on in this land. Look here, Captain. The troopers will finish up the burying of Perdition Springs' dead, and I'll read some scripture over the graves. That's our obligation to these unfortunate souls. But then this company is going to move out after those renegades, never mind the kind of start they have. Never mind that they're at home in these desert flats and hills. Already our scouts are combing the flats for sign of what direction the savages took. And if we manage to engage — "

The tall major let his sentence hang, but Jenks Wilcox recognized determination like his own. As he turned away from the scorched, mutilated corpse of Beauregard Lee, he couldn't help shaking his head in disbelief. The officer's mind raced. *To wind up meeting such an end. Goddamn!* And then a final thought came before he replaced his expired cigar. *Lord, though, but that man was a wizard at chess!*

They trailed up out of the Perdition Springs dish, following the tracks of unshod ponies — the raiders' ponies. It was a hellish ride through more malpais country, barren of all but the most hardy desert plants, barren of active animal life during the day as well. The scorpions and sidewinders had retreated to ground cracks and the shade of rocks. The only water apparent was a mirage, an ever-tantalizing, pure-blue crystal lake shimmering in the distance.

The Buffalo Soldiers slouched in the butt-bruising McClellans, mouthing low complaints. But their eyes were ever alert to scan horizons for dust clouds, or watch an occasional ash-fleck of buzzard as it soared on high. Wilcox had ordered out his flank riders in addition to the Mescalero scouts. He took as few chances as possible, although any adventure in this country outside a fort's walls was a large gamble indeed. An ambush could take place almost anywhere. Gullies and draws laced the brutal terrain, and the Apaches were shrewd stalkers — the best in the world.

The situation was enough to give a soldier pause, but Jenks Wilcox and Marcus Cavanaugh refused to linger. The trail led into foothills and over ancient lava beds. And then in the hard and reddish underfoot, there were no more tracks — or even horse droppings. First Sergeant Labe Meadow had taken the Mescalero scout's report, and relayed it to the officers.

"Before he rode on up ahead again, he say the raiders' ponies ain't been eatin' much nor drinkin', so neither do they shit. Scouts kind of reckon as how we've lost 'em."

"Goddamn," Jenks Wilcox growled.

"This might have been expected, Captain," Marcus said. "But you can use the company for combing as we head back toward Fort Bowie. The odds are no worse for turning up Nantaje that way, than on regular patrol."

"We're to head on back?"

"The company has limited rations. You can't drift far from the dependable springs and tanks this time of year. But first, I have a mission at San Carlos, remember. To deliver the word to Chief Gleheehaco, of the coming railroad's taking reservation lands."

"The agency isn't far from where we are now, isn't that right?" Jenks Wilcox conned the dazzling sky and the ominous sawtooth hills shouldering in the north-west.

"Fifteen miles. We can bivouac there tonight. There are some trees and shade. Hopefully the reservation Apaches won't get overly upset at the news I'll be delivering."

"Isn't that rather a faint hope, Major?"

Marcus' smile was less than cheerful. "You're correct on that score, Captain. I consider Gleheehaco a good Indian friend, but he's an old man. There are plenty of younger would-be leaders looking for a chance to gain influence. This damn Interior Department decision just might set them off."

"And when the warrior bucks are triggered to become broncos, then it's — ?"

"Hell to pay, Wilcox. Hell to pay."

There was a waving signal from a scout perched on a distant rise. Marcus and Wilcox kicked their mounts to motion. The closed-up column commenced to move, too.

They trudged wearily across the forbidding tawny landscape under the sky's vast dome. And the sun hammered all.

Chapter Fifteen

"It is a very wrong thing, what you speak of, Marcus Cavanaugh," Gleheehaco said.

The old Mimbres Apache chief wore a motley combination of white man's and Indian garb, common on the reservation, complete with an ancient slouch hat long discarded by some trooper. The chief's gray hair framed a seamed bronze visage, unusually mobile now in its expression of displeasure. The major and Gleheehaco sat close together, face-to-face in the center of the wickiup. The door flap was in place, and they were quite alone.

Marcus squirmed his rump on the cushion of piled skins and returned the gaze from two eyes that were black as coal chips. The preliminaries of conversation had been gotten through, a few jokes exchanged, the routine greetings expressing the men's courtesy. Then Marcus had told what Hiram Titus and General Grummond had decreed. The Indian wasn't taking it at all well.

Personally, Marcus felt the old chief's assessment was correct. Crowding the seven or more tribes, all traditional foes, still more closely together in the gravelly desert bottom along San Carlos Creek, the act was wrong indeed. The huntable game had long since fled the region — although every vile native insect had remained. The dry, baked soil resisted every attempt at Agency-directed farming. The people subsisted on weekly doles of flour and beef.

Always the rations turned out a bit short, so malnutrition weighed heavily upon the elderly and the young.

The Apaches hated their lives on the reservation, and the threat of them breaking from its confines was very real.

"I have told you what the White Fathers have said, Gleheehaco," Marcus assured the chief. "These are the things that the Apaches must submit to."

"Our life is hard in this place. There is sickness, and too many of the People die of it."

"It is the way the peaceful Apache must live."

The parchmentlike skin of the chief's face was stretched taut. He smelled old, and he was frail in his years, his days of battle exploits far in the past.

"There was a time, Marcus Cavanaugh," he now started to expound, "when the Mimbres People wandered far on the mountains and across the flats. Gleheehaco was a great leader of warriors on raids. The Maricopas and the Yavapai and the Pima all knew to flee us. We took much loot and many women to be our wives or slaves. Then the ones called the Mexicans came to our lands. We fought them. Then the White Eyes settlers and the soldier bluecoats. Many young men of the Mimbres were killed in war."

Gleheehaco's reedy voice droned on. "Our young warriors, they died bravely," he intoned. "They were never cowards, but still they are dead and gone. The

138

People were not vanquished, but we grew weary of the fight. Ever more White Eyes kept coming from beyond the rising sun. So Gleheehaco, he made an agreement with the White Eyes war leader, General Grummond. The Mimbrenos would put their rifles down, come to dwell on this poor, small piece of ground. Gleheehaco has never broken his promise to the white General Grummond."

"I know it, Chief. I know."

"Now our young men waste their days at gambling and singing sad songs of the old days when the People were free. Our women gather hay for the White Eyes agency police's horses, this to earn a few pennies. We are told of laws to be obeyed — and what are these things called 'laws'? We are not to brew *tiswin*! If a wife is unfaithful, her husband cannot cut off her nose!"

"The peaceful Apache must live so," Marcus said.

Gleheehaco drew his emaciated frame up straight. "You talk of peaceful Apaches, Marcus Cavanaugh. All of us here are not such, not in our stomachs and livers and hearts. There are young men at San Carlos who don't want to be here! The ties that hold them are weak. They have poor weapons, and they have no bold leaders! But what you bluecoats don't know is, Nantaje himself has been here! He promises new rifles for those who would follow him! He promises much loot and the spilling of White Eyes blood!"

Marcus prompted the old red man. "Nantaje promises that the white settlers and the white army will be driven out if the young men of all tribes fight the soldiers together? Mimbrenos and Coyoteros and Ariraipas and Warm Springs Apaches, although the bands have been enemies to each other since the grandfather times?"

"These are the promises. Yes, Marcus Cavanaugh."

"And the Mimbreno bucks, they believe Nantaje?

Gleeheehaco nodded his ancient, gray head. "Nantaje's medicine is said to be strong. I — " He thumped his chest till his brass reservation-number tag bounced. "I no longer control the young men. They don't want to be friends to Marcus Cavanaugh!"

The major's gaze roamed the squalid hut's interior. A few straw baskets stood about, plus an emptied foodstuffs box, now repacked with religious talismans and herbs. There was an old berrywood bow reinforced with stag's horn. Marcus doubted the chief's strength now to pull and shoot with it. The wickiup was filled with futile memories.

If the young bucks no longer respected the old chief, Marcus thought, what was the point in trying? Nevertheless, try he did.

"Gleeheehaco, what if Nantaje's renegades are beaten by the soldiers? What if Nantaje himself were killed? It would prove, then, to all, that the Chiricahua bronco's medicine is not strong, but weak?"

A solemn nod. "But, of course, Marcus Cavanaugh."

"Urge your tribe's young men to wait, Gleeheehaco. Nantaje will be defeated soon. He will meet many brave army soldiers, some are white, but some have skins that are brown or black. Against the soldiers and their guns, Nantaje's bronco warriors can't stand fast. They will all be killed, or else brought back in chains for all the wrongs they've done."

The old chief grunted. "Nantaje spoke powerfully when he came to this place. The young men believed him. I do not think, Marcus Cavanaugh, that they will believe you. They will want to see proof."

"Then, it's important that I supply proof," Marcus said, rising. "Now, Chief, it's time for me to go. The Buffalo Soldiers wait below the agency. We will ride together to pursue Nantaje, for he has wiped out the town of Perdition Springs."

Gleheehaco shrugged. "This is something I know nothing of."

"Take my advice, chief. Persuade your young men not to ride to war."

This time there was no answer from Gleheehaco. Marcus rose and left the wickiup, allowing the deerskin flap to close behind him silently.

As he stalked through the shabby rancheria to where he'd tied his horse, he received some hostile looks from idle, gaunt Mimbres men. He mounted quickly and guided his bay through a few alders along the shallow creek. At the foot of the slope, amid a towering upheaval of boulders, he rejoined Company E.

"It didn't go well?" queried Jenks Wilcox.

"Did you really expect it would?"

"No."

"You were right. Have the troopers mount up to ride, Captain. I think it best we return to Bowie through the mountains. There's a possibility of a message from Nantaje for me."

"I heard at the fort about Harry Gougan and his Indian wife. Are Nantaje and his sister really that close?"

"Hardly." Marcus drew his gauntlets on his hands, straightened his hat. "But reaching him through her still may be the only chance we'll ever get."

The desert twilight had lowered on Fort Bowie. The lamps in the windows of the buildings that flanked the compounds threw innumerable pools of yellow light. Supper done with, the men idled about in the last few hours before taps, some strolling the paths, others drinking grog at the sutlers' bars. In the enlisted men's barracks, a mouth organ wailed. From one of the houses on married officers' row, a harmonium pumped a cheerful tune.

On the roofed, railed porch of Captain and Mrs. Frye's dwelling, deep shadows curtained vision. There a couple stood engaged in soft conversation.

"But now is a good time, and here's a good place to talk," came a masculine nasal whine. Moody Pearson's long suits were barbering, clothes, and diamond stickpins. Those, and his lean, distinguished face. As long as he'd been rich, he'd never met a woman who complained about his voice.

"Well, if you think so, Moody." Sophia Frye wasn't too sure, but she let herself be led. "Supper's over, and Shelby has gone back to headquarters and his monthly requisitions."

"The captain has played into our hands." The railroad man gave a practiced chuckle. "This is the chance I've been awaiting, dear Sophia, to say how much I've come to care. On this bleak journey since departing Atchison, I've found no woman who affects me like you. Ma'am, you're a gem, a sweet flower blooming in a wild land. Don't let it continue to be your fate when you don't need to!"

"Well, I didn't always live on the frontier. There were the years in Washington I spent with Shelby — "

"The man's a scoundrel for transplanting you out here! Unworthy of a sensitive woman's love. Ah, Sophia, don't say you love him! I know better!"

"The happy hours lately have been few, that's true."

"Naturally."

Moody Pearson dabbed moist lips with a handkerchief of linen. Meanwhile, his hand crept over to cover that of the adjutant's wife. "Captain Frye's wrapped up in career. Not that he's a success at the military life. Aged forty-five, and still merely a captain! He's on a treadmill. Unfit ever to be given a real command."

"Well-l — "

The silhouettes in the evening darkness seemed to merge. Moody Pearson's lips sought the ripe ones of Sophia. The broadcloth of his frock coat caressed her arms below her dress sleeves. His brocade vest pressed her heaving bodice. "Sophia, my dear!"

Along the path in his house's dark shadow, Captain Shelby Frye hurried, bustling. Having forgotten papers that he needed at the office, he'd been forced to make this quick jaunt home. At the corner beside the plot of cultivated tamarisks, however, he threw himself against the clapboard wall and froze. He heard voices. Familiar voices.

The captain prepared to eavesdrop.

The woman's voice was muffled, as if breaking off a kiss. "Goodness me! Mr. Pearson!"

"Call me Moody. Sophia, I'll be leaving for the East with Mr. Titus in just a few more days. Our duties are through out here. Perhaps you'll return with me. It's my hope you will. But let's make the most of now, shall we? Let me join you in your boudoir. Tonight? Now?"

Shelby Frye started forward, a flush of anger tinge-ing his face between his sideburns. He forced himself to freeze again. He wanted to witness the next developments. Sophia was pushing from the man who'd been seeking to invade her bed. "I can't!" she bleated. "Not now! Perhaps not ever! I-I need t-to think!"

"I must warn you to make up your mind soon," Moody Pearson said huskily. "Let me only state this. Were your husband an army hero, then staying with him might make sense. But as it is, Frye's a desk officer, and destined to remain one. And now, Sophia, good night!"

Shelby Frye slammed his fist into his palm, his face contorting in a futile rage. But he made no move to mount the porch or go inside. His wife was there alone, but now was not the time to confront her.

Frye turned on his heel, and hurried back in the direction of headquarters.

Harry Gougan stepped out of his mountain cabin to confront the fresh new morning. A cactus wren sang in the ocotillo, and a jackrabbit bolted across the yard. The morning was, as usual, clear and fine. The sun's rays were bright through the alders and the pinyons. His pretty wife, though, was nowhere to be seen. "Sentagolatha," the giant former scout called in mock gruffness. On the patch of bare earth in front of his doorway he paused to stretch his thick arms and back. The seams of his shirt almost, but not quite, burst. "Sentagolatha, kitten?"

From the pine motte beside the dwelling stepped four burly human forms. As quietly as ghosts, they fanned out behind the giant of a man. The squat ones had Apache builds — and the characteristic scowls. "We have been looking for the woman also," the foremost Indian of the group snarled fiercely. "Where has she gone, Man Mountain?"

"Christ! Chiricahuas!" Harry Gougan dove into action, throwing himself to one side, spinning, clawing a huge hand to jerk his six-gun clear.

"Take him alive, my brothers," Nantaje snapped. Gougan's Colt boomed, but missed its bolting target.

The Apaches charged.

Chapter Sixteen

Harry Gougan looked left, then quickly charged side-long from his position in the yard. Already the broncos from Nantaje's band had cut off all retreat toward the cabin. The giant again triggered his six-gun from the crouch he'd assumed — once, then twice — and the two closest Apaches were fetched up at the slam of 200-grain slugs. Both spun aside and dropped heavily to earth. More ran from the trees to take their places.

Gougan remained alive because Nantaje had commanded that he not be shot. What he didn't know was the war leader's reasoning. But there was no point in surviving an onslaught by the bastards, for they'd kill him in the end — and that would be slow. But he vowed to slay as many as he could, while he could. And only then face what was going to take place after.

A warrior collided with him, and he breathed the savage's heavy smell. The pair wrestled briefly, and then the giant hurled the redskin off and fired a bullet into him. The gut-wounded bronco plowed into a companion, and both fell down. Mongash came at Harry

145

Gougan with a war club swinging. Gougan shot Mongash's jaw away. The warrior dropped, his face spouting gouts of blood.

"Take the Man Mountain alive!" again came Nantaje's shout in Chiricahua. Three cord-muscled warriors closed in from all sides. Harry Gougan had been counting cartridges as he used them. He had one round left.

There was no real thought of using it on himself. He aimed past the closest closing warrior at Nantaje. The ferocious, yelling savage was in his sights. Gougan triggered.

A miss!

One warrior hit Harry Gougan high, one hit him low, bowling him over onto the rich green grama.

Gougan plucked his twelve-inch Bowie knife from its sheath, and sheathed it again — in his squirming antagonist's chest. The Apache grunted and died. Gougan was jumped on as he rolled on the ground. Harsh pain exploded in his privates. A fisted rock struck his head, and then again against in his bearded jaw. Blazing agony welled down to his collarbone. Fireworks pinwheeled in his brain, but he fought off blacking out.

He jabbed with his blade, and an opponent's arm was slit elbow to wrist. Flooding blood spattered shirts, skin, faces. Gougan gritted his teeth and fought on. Strong Apache bucks attempted to pin the big man, but Gougan possessed strength, too. His massive body owned tremendous endurance for punishment.

He pumped up a knee and flung a bronco into a sprawling somersault. Lashing out with a boot toe, he mauled another Apache's ear. The struggle was fought in grim silence, the only sounds being scuffling dirt and a few hoarse grunts. There was a great kicking of muscular legs. Sweat sprouted from the bearded giant's face and streamed down. Sprawled as he was, sat on, even

146

sledged with stones, Harry Gougan at last felt his tremendous strength ebbing.

Channeling all his reserve power into a final move, he bucked upward, arching his torso at the same time that he flailed out with both arms. The two Apaches on his chest tumbled into the grass. Swinging up his legs, he locked them around a third struggling warrior. He squeezed mightily, and the breath fled from tormented lungs. The warrior's features changed from copper to blue.

Gougan bunched his knuckles and drove them into the Apache's jaw.

Momentarily freed, the giant rolled to his feet, only to confront yet another Indian. Nantaje himself. But the contest was unfair. The warrior held a stout bow, and was notching an arrow. With a great roar of rage, the white man threw himself at the war leader.

Nantaje drew back the bow string and stood poised a split second. Every straining muscle cord in his shoulders, arms, and back sprang forth in outline. The feathered, steel-tipped missile flew. The arrow drove deep into the flesh of Harry Gougan's thigh, lodging there. The pain was horrendous. The big man catapulted from his feet and landed headfirst, heavily.

"Ha! Grab the White Eyes! Drag him up!" Nantaje tossed Cosotee's bow back to the young warrior, then ran close, and wrapped a hand in Gougan's flaming beard. "You married the sister that I now despise, Man Mountain," he snarled. "She lives in your *cho-sa*. You must know where she is now. You will tell Nantaje!"

"No!"

"Sentagolatha told Noohatacah in the rancheria that the bluecoat major wants to talk! Nantaje spits on the bluecoat major! But if I command it, the woman will go and lie, lie to all the White Eyes, and the pony soldiers will come to Thunderhorse! When they come, Nantaje's warriors will kill all of them!"

"Bushwhackin' Injun bastard!"

Nantaje's hand gripped the haft of the arrow that extended from Harry Gougan's leg. He gave it a vicious wrench. The big man bit back the excruciating stab of pain, but his entire frame spasmed. When he opened the eyes he'd squeezed shut, he saw Nantaje's knife under his nose. "Nantaje will scalp Man Mountain's beard unless he talks! Very much hurting of Man Mountain! Now, where has gone the woman Sentagolatha this day?"

Harry Gougan said nothing.

Nantaje gestured with a hand and sneered.

The bearded giant was hurled roughly to the ground by surrounding Chiricahuas. Out came the binding cords and stakes. They pinioned him faceup on a small, unshaded hillock a short distance from the trees. The stretched muscles in his limbs ached and throbbed. The wounded thigh was a bolt of molten fire.

The victim's clothes were torn off, and the torture commenced, first on the extremities. Thorns were shoved under toe and fingernails. One by one the fingers were bent back and broken. They made it last almost an hour. Gougan couldn't help flinching when the pain was worst, but he refused to scream. The devilish work went on in horrible silence, the red men taking turns.

The moment came when Nantaje understood. Gougan wouldn't tell them Sentagolatha's whereabouts. The mountain man cherished his wife.

Nantaje grunted something to the warrior called Pamitoohai, "Antelope Prong." Now that no information was to be expected from the Man Mountain, they could proceed with devilish fun. Deftly wielded knives pared strips of skin from the hairy, quivering chest. Fire to Harry Gougan's foot soles turned the tender flesh first pink, then purplish-red.

Harry Gougan showed no pain. He had lived among the Comanches as a boy. His will was strong.

Several warriors emerged from the cabin door, having conducted a quick interior search. With them they bore a smoking iron scuttle containing coals from Gougan's coffee fire. The prize was shown to Nantaje.

Nantaje smiled.

The wicked glee never left the war leader's face as he crouched close to Harry Gougan's head. A viselike hand across the cheeks and nose pressed the head back, and held it motionless. Gougan could feel and smell the nearby heat of coals, but he made no sound. He felt an eyelid pried open and saw a trade knife's sharp point descend. It hurt like hell when Nantaje carved out the eyeball.

Even as the blood ran, Harry Gougan wouldn't cry out.

Only within his head did the words flood his half-crazed mind: *Oh, God! Oh, God! Oh, God! Oh, God!* Nantaje grinned. He balanced a single smoking-hot coal on his blade. The coal glowed a bright cherry-red. Nantaje thrust the cherry coal into Gougan's empty eye socket.

Gougan twitched and flopped like hooked fish on a line. He broke silence shrilly: "Yaaa! Yaaa! Yaaa! Yaaa-aaaah!"

At that moment, there was shouting from somewhere in the woods. Then, Geehoho, "Fat Otter," ran into the glade, dragging Sentagolatha by her long skein of unbound raven hair. With a powerful arm swipe the warrior shoved the stumbling woman forward. She sprawled beside Nantaje's moccasins.

"She was beyond the low hills," the warrior explained. "Gathering berries!"

"Ah!"

Sentagolatha caught sight of her naked, tortured, screaming husband. She wailed.

The war leader spent no words on preliminaries. "My sister," he scolded. "Now you will help the Chiricahuas and Nantaje! Go to the White Eyes major, tell him we shall meet as he wants! Our warriors will wait for the bluecoats near Thunderhorse, in the canyon called Trap. Nantaje will see all the bluecoats slain, and laugh!".

"You torture my husband, and then want my help? Nantaje, you are 'mind-flown-away'!"

"You will not help the People?"

"I will never help you!"

The trading knife's razor blade flashed, then buried deep above the woman's bulging abdomen. "You've killed my baby!" she gasped, her face contorting. "Y-you've killed . . . me!" She sagged downward, dead before she hit the ground.

Harry Gougan's lusty screams had turned weak, thin, ululating. The big man's strength was fading fast.

"Slice off Man Mountain's manhood member," Nantaje directed. "It is time for us to go from this place!"

By the time ponies were brought up, all that could be heard were a few pitiful wails. The Chiricahuas rode off without a backward glance.

Marcus Cavanaugh rode with Jenks Wilcox at the head of E Company, the column strung out behind under the tall pines that lined the trail. The horses had been climbing for hours into the mountains, and still they climbed. It was the officers' plan to reach the Gougans' spread before nightfall, and bivouac near the sweet, cool spring. If Sentagolatha could be encouraged to do her utmost with Nantaje, Marcus felt, the leader of raids might be shown his foolishness. Even with a war

150

party augmented from the San Carlos tribes, he could not win in the end. The United States Army would go on fighting, especially with the arrival of railroad construction crews. There could only be more pointless death meted out, mostly to Apaches. The time for them to make treaty with the White Eyes' fathers was now, not later.

"Do you figure the couple will be at the ranch?" Jenks Wilcox wondered. "Not gone off somewhere?"

"Gougan's usually at home." Marcus scanned the trail up the long, rock-bound incline. The Mescalero scouts were out there, sent to range well ahead. They should have reached the spread, looked the place over, and by now be doubling back in order to report.

The leaders of the troop rode out of the slotlike canyon and rounded an enormous, loaf-shaped granite barrier. Ahead lay tumbled boulders, interspersed with dark green pines. There was a notch in a ridge, and in it one of the Mescalero riders. Marcus recognized the bandy-legged one called Desalin, quite a reliable man. Desalin's arm waved with his carbine aloft. It foretold trouble.

"See it?" Marcus asked Wilcox.

"I see him, Major."

The officers gave spur, and the weary horses bolted ahead, to be reined in at the scarp.

"Trouble?"

The scout grunted. "Plenty trouble. The mountain man and his woman, both are dead. Nantaje's work."

"Call the column forward at the lope, Captain," Marcus ordered. They advanced up the trail with their weapons at ready.

The final pine grove caused the trail to wind. The soldiers bent low in their McClellans and ducked their heads to avoid low branches. The fresh scent of firs was overlaid now with an unforgettable sickly stench. Marcus had smelled it before. Scorched flesh. Captain Wilcox rode at his side again, the hawkish nose thrust out, his features frozen and grim. There was a murmuring back among the Buffalo Soldiers. They were smelling the stench now, too.

The cabin broke into view, and then the clearing. Marcus' big bay horse shied at the strong smell of spilled blood. And then, through the brush, he glimpsed the woman's huddled corpse, then Gougan's spreadeagled one.

Back down the line a trooper gagged and retched.

Marcus, Wilcox, and Desalin reined in. Mescalero scouts stood about, blank-faced; all the soldiers' gazes were fixed on the horrible butchery.

Chapter Seventeen

The three-man burial detail had done its work, and the stock had been set free from the pole corral. A bit more than an hour had passed since E Company had ridden in, and the sun was no longer high over the spread that the retired scout Gougan had carved from the wilderness. It was the all-too-fleeting time of twilight in the mountain fastness, and Marcus Cavanaugh sat on a stump. He stroked his jaw and considered what to do next.

The company was technically under the command of Captain Wilcox, but the junior officer, new to Apache fighting, seemed to be looking to him — Marcus — as a guide to correct action now. The pair of officers had agreed that the Mescalero scouts should prowl the area. The route the Chiricahua raiders had taken when they left — that information was going to hold the key to what came next. If the band had split up, there'd be no telling which of several groups Nantaje accompanied. If, however, the single large band had stayed together, there was a chance they could track him down.

First Sergeant Labe Meadow's regulation boots rustled in the pine needles as he approached. "A couple of the scouts, they're back now, suh," the stocky black man said, saluting. "They'll be joinin' you and the captain here in a minute."

"Right. I'll be waiting."

Marcus had made it a point to get to know the Mescaleros by name, and as they crossed the glade in their usual mile-gobbling shuffle, he recognized Desalin and an older, pock-faced Indian named Skibahete. Both were sinister-looking individuals, but Lieutenant Neel, the commander of the scout company, swore by them. Both had fought bravely in past skirmishes and carried out tough missions.

Most important for the moment, Desalin and Skibahete were experts at reading sign — the best in the troop.

Skibahete chose to do the talking. "Marcus Cavanaugh, we have found the Chiricahua raiders' trail down from this mountain place. They ride their ponies all together. They do not break up in smaller groups. And this band it is a big one, mebbe sixty or seventy warriors. There must be men of the People from several tribes who have joined Nantaje to raid and loot. It is the biggest band of warriors Nantaje has ever led."

Jenks Wilcox shook his head in surprise. "That's a lot of broncos in one great big bunch, Major. Are you thinking what I'm thinking?"

"Undoubtedly, Captain." Turning to the scout, Marcus asked crisply, "Skibahete, in which direction are the broncos traveling?"

"Nantaje's force rides south."

"Would they be difficult to track?"

"Easy to track! They have no more than a few hours' start. Easy for Mescalero scouts, mebbe not white officers or black-skinned Buffalo Soldiers!"

"That tears it! They must be heading for Thunderhorse!"

"Yes," Skibahete said. "Thunderhorse, big mesa of the spirit ghosts. Haunted mesa. Nantaje will not climb the place of vengeful dead, but near there the Chiricahua rancherias are well hidden. Much hard-to-travel ground. Deep barrancas to hide in."

"Can our scouts find them?"

"Mescalaros find."

"Done!"

Jenks Wilcox remained puzzled. "What's being decided here, Major? It would be good to trap this big force Nantaje leads, break its back before we get more massacres like Perdition Springs."

"We agree, Captain. We agree. You're in charge of the troop, of course, and I'm a tagalong on this trip. However, I recommend you not miss this opportunity for hot pursuit. Let the company rest tonight, and let our horses rest. We can set out in the morning, early. Maybe we'll be able to gain on them. Down near Thunderhorse we'll try to box them in and do battle. Meanwhile — "

"Yes, Major? Go on."

"I suggest sending a dispatch rider off to Fort Bowie. He should start out immediately to report Nantaje's observed direction and where he'll end up. Request a reinforcement squadron from the garrison to rendezvous with us there. Then, if we do succeed in forcing an engagement on the hostiles — cut them off so they must stand and fight — our side will have the numbers to make a decisive defeat. It's the best opportunity that the Army's had in years, Captain! And it just may be our last opportunity!"

"I'll issue the orders right away."

"You do that." To Desalin and Skibahete, Marcus added, "You'll let the rest of the scouts know our plan as

155

soon as they report in. You'll be ready at first light to lead us on Nantaje's trail."

"Yes, Marcus Cavanaugh!" Within minutes, cook fires were flaring about the bivouac area, and canvas tents were being thrown up. Marcus sighed. It could be the last wet camp and the last warm camp they'd all be seeing for a while. Down on the desert it could be unwise to show nighttime light or daytime smoke. And if Nantaje were poisoning the water holes, there would be quite a few strong thirsts in E Company throats.

The lanky major peered up at night's indigo, winking curtain. The stars hung above the treetops, beautiful and serene. Harry Gougan and Sentagolatha would never spoon again beneath that sheeting blaze of stars. The thought was a sad one. But this time, finally, Nantaje's string of luck might just have run short!

By noon of the second day, the forced march was telling severely on the mounts and men. E Company, Buffalo Soldiers, sat on their saddles stiffly, butts aching from the pounding they'd absorbed. Hats, kerchiefs, uniform blouses were coated with whitish-saffron dust. So were the skins of bare faces and hands. Both officers and enlisted men appeared drenched in stage makeup — the kind actors used to portray ghosts in plays.

Only the dauntless Apache scouts were unaffected by short water and short rations. They'd been raised since boyhood in the practice of restricting their drink and food. And they'd been trained to run from dawn to dusk in knee-high moccasins. The Mescaleros were faring satisfactorily, for to them this was business as usual. Life in the desert. Make it, or die.

When they led the way into the sink under the beetling brows of Thunderhorse, they seemed energetic as ever, even eager. They'd reported to their officers that Nantaje's party hadn't yet divided — and was unlikely to. Although the Chiricahuas had to have seen the column's dust cloud on their back trail, they'd kept going on their way toward home. Either they had confidence in the strength of their cliff-locked strongholds, or contempt for the bluecoats. But the third alternative was that the soldiers were being led into a deadly trap.

The Mescalero scouts knew, Marcus Cavanaugh knew, and Captain Jenks Wilcox knew from the sketchy maps he'd been shown, that Thunderhorse Mesa was a place of forbidding and secretive heights. And its approaches contained badland tracts among the worst on the continent. Broken-down escarpments, jumbles of giant rock slabs — cracked, splintered, gouged by eons of scouring winds. Granite, basalt, and sandstone scale had been hewn by the elements in a host of fantastic formations, and between these the land was gashed by steep ravines. The mesa itself was an enormous, vertical-faced bluff columned with buff and red monoliths.

Through this virtually impassable terrain, the troops would need to pass in order to bring the dreaded war leader, Nantaje, to heel.

The soldiers heard the the harsh, grating voice of Jenks Wilcox ringing. "Company prepare to rest! Di-i-is- *mount!*"

The jaded men stepped from leather and dropped immediately to their backsides, clutching canteens. There was a swift round of whistle-wetting, and cheap stogies were hastily lit.

"See any of our scouts?" Wilcox questioned Marcus. The major tugged off his campaign hat and shook his head.

"But we're getting into dangerous ambush terrain. They're doing some tall sniffing, you may be sure, out among those mysterious hills. Captain, I want to congratulate you on the hardiness of your men. This is a grueling march, and they're standing up to it."

"They're Buffalo Soldiers, Major Cavanaugh. Tough, skilled fighting men."

"They'll stand up well against the Chiricahua raiders, I predict."

"I know that, sir. I've known it since first setting foot in this hell."

Marcus laughed. "You sound ready to ride on into those badlands that we face, Captain. Desalin and Skibahete claim that the renegades' rancherias are down close to the mesa's base. There's said to be a barranca — a gorge — that's well-nigh impassable, and therefore highly defensible. We can wait for our reinforcements to arrive, but then we risk the possibility of the raiders' getting out the other end. If they lead all their families off into Mexico, they're out of our reach, but could go right on with their hit-and-run raiding ways."

"But if we ride right on in after them, we risk an ambush."

"You read the situation correctly, mister."

"Meadow will have the column mounted in a minute. Then I say forward ho."

The company entered the walled canyon, and rode down into a windless ovenlike hotbox filled with boulders from the rim. Every crumbling rock radiated heat like a stove top. The mounts plodded through fetlock-deep detritus, and the going grew painfully slow. Every quarter mile, Marcus paused to sweep the rims and walls with field glasses. He saw no signs of life — not even animal life. This in itself was an unnatural sign, he was given to understand.

When a flock of magpies winged wheeling upward from a distant outcrop, Desalin explained that the birds had been frightened into flight.

"Apaches?" A grim nod.

"Then, they're up there?"

"Still on the move, yes, Major Cavanaugh. But as they go, they leave lookouts. They are watching us."

"But if we don't proceed, we can never overtake the main party?"

"That is true."

"Then we'll ride on."

The sun was sinking down in the western sky when a sudden shot rang out. Instantly, the troopers' hands were on their carbines' stocks, unbooting. The heavy, breech-loading .45-70 singleshots were fingered edgily. Eyes searched the cliffs for further puffs of smoke. Ahead, a vee was cut in the rocks by a stream, now dry. Above the vee a smear of gunsmoke hovered.

"We'll ride on through, shooting!" Jenks Wilcox decided. "We can get past their small rear guard! The main party's gone on ahead! Trumpeter, sound the charge!"

It was probably a good tactic, Marcus thought. Were it up to him, he'd be issuing the same commands. Once through the narrow stretch, the column would have cut off the bronco guards from the main party and Nantaje, their chief. Skirmishers ought to be able to flush out the enemy, pick them off. There seemed no way for the hostiles to scamper up those precipices.

The trumpeter bounced his call off the echoing walls.

The galloping horseflesh piled on through, officers in the lead, side arms drawn and cocked.

Then all hell broke loose.

From the cliffs erupted a heavy fusillade, the reports of rifles crackling like strings of Chinese firecrackers. Red-orange flashes speared the air on high, not many, but enough. The ambushers' fire was taking a toll. Up and down the column several troopers were wounded by slugs.

"Return fire!" shouted Captain Wilcox, spurring his horse.

"Fire at will!" seconded Sergeant Meadow, bellowing.

The Springfield 'charcoal furnaces' began to boom. The canyon was filled with drifting acrid smoke.

Galloping toward the notch, Marcus found it hard to see. But then he saw a sight that chilled him, and heard some equally unwelcome sounds.

There was a roar of concentrated Winchester fire. Bullets beat the surrounding weathered rocks. One slug found Jenks Wilcox, and the officer was punched half around in his saddle. Crimson blood blossomed on the dark blue blouse. The rider slumped, but was prevented from falling by Meadow, whose massive arm encircled the wounded officer.

"He's hit bad, Major!" Meadow yelled.

Marcus threw up his left hand. "Listen to me then, men! Renew the charge! On through the notch, there! Fire and keep firing! Give the savages pure hell!"

The bugle call took up again.

The Buffalo Soldiers thundered down the canyon, a furious, hurtling avalanche.

Chapter Eighteen

"Who goes there?"

"Private Rufus Stewart, Mister Sentry-on-the-Wall! E Company!"

"Buffalo Soldier?"

"Bet your ass!"

The trooper on Fort Bowie's parapet peered down at the black man straddling the stumbling, sweat-coated horse. "You look like you been ridin' through hell, soldier. Get that mount of yours on in through the gate, and take your message to headquarters!"

Stewart rolled his eyes at the blazing sky, and kicked the rawboned bay through the post entrance. For a change, the American flag was snapping at its staff as Stewart rode across the parade ground. No fewer than three figures emerged from the low building opposite to stand on the broad, white veranda.

Stewart stepped from leather and hurried to the steps. "Sergeant Major Brody, sir? Private Stewart, E Company, reporting in after a pure devil of a ride!"

The paunchy Irishman snapped a return salute. "It does appear that it was, lad, by the auld sod! And what's been happenin' to good Captain Wilcox?"

Stewart rolled out a swift, accurate account of the Gougan couple's fate. "The captain and the major, they're lettin' the scouts follow along the raiders' trail. Down the badlands way, in front of Thunderhorse. Know where that is?"

"Aye. And the column'll be wantin' some relief? Officers'll need to be told. Colonel Thornhill, he happens to be occupied just now. Here's Captain Frye, though. He's the adjutant. Acts as exec when Major Cavanaugh's away."

The trooper brushed streaming sweat from his brow. "They be wantin' that relief squadron soon, Sergeant!"

Frye descended the whitewashed steps. Hiram Titus, suited and flushed, hurried at his side. "What's going on? Some kind of emergency?"

"E Company's hot on Nantaje's trail, sir. There's a passel o' renegades, and a chance to pin 'em down and wipe 'em out. Captain Wilcox, he respectfully submits — "

"Colonel Thornhill has to know this, and immediately," Hiram Titus put in. "Where's the post commander now, Captain Frye? And for that matter, where's Moody Pearson?"

"I have my ideas about both men, Mr. Titus," Frye said. Bitterness edged his tone, but he wore a shark's grin. "Pearson and his doings are of little account to me just now, but the colonel, that's another matter. I'll go 'round and deliver this news personally. Oh, and Mr. Titus, perhaps you should accompany me. You're a Washington official. Step this way, please, along this boardwalk."

No one had ordered Brody not to trail them, so the sergeant major quietly dropped into step. It didn't take long. They were at the commander's doorstep in a few short minutes. Frye rapped gently at first on the oak panel.

"Colonel? Are you in there? There's a message from the field, and — " The hard pounding sent the door opening inward on silent hinges. The draperies were drawn, and the room was dim with filtered light. Excited by the news he bore, Frye proceeded to the center of the parlor, paused, and cast his gaze about. Hiram Titus shuffled edgily to his side.

Brody waited in the doorway, backlit by the sun.

"Nothing to be seen," Titus rasped softly. The pudgy hands at the government man's sides clasped and unclasped nervously.

"Nothing but this." The polished toe of Frye's Jefferson boot nudged an empty whiskey bottle. "I'm going to look in the other rooms."

They found the colonel in the bedroom, on his mattress, foggily rousing himself. He seemed surprised at being disturbed. "What's going on — ?" Thornhill's voice was growling and slurred. "W-wassamatter? C-captain Frye?" Thornhill's blouse was flecked with sputum, and his iron-gray hair was mussed. Worse, his breath stank of whiskey.

Hiram Titus wrinkled his flat, fat nose. "Thornhill! Indeed!" was his indignant snort. "You appear unable to take command of an important matter that's come up."

"There's a runner come in from the field, Colonel," Frye stated, talking rapidly. "Something about Cavanaugh and Wilcox and Wilcox's company. They have a chance at Nantaje. A decisive chance."

Frank Thornhill's face flushed as he struggled from the bed. "Th-they're going t' need re-reinforcements. D-damn me, where's m' bloody h-hat — "

The words weren't finished because his foot slipped and he crashed to the bedroom floor. The lolling head

163

slammed the base of the applewood chiffonier. Colonel Thornhill rolled on his side, knocked out cold.

"Good God," cried Titus.

Frye said: "I possess the top brevet rating on this entire post! I'm taking command! Sergeant Major Brody!"

"Yessir!"

"Have the trumpeter sound call to arms! I'll want a squadron of three companies to take to the field! A Company! C Company! F Company! With a compliment of Apache scouts to guide me to this Thunderhorse place!"

"You, sir?"

"I'll be in command, yes!"

"But — "

"Do as I order, sergeant!"

Brody scuttled away.

"Come along now, Mr. Titus. I'll ask the surgeon to step around and care for Colonel Thornhill. You'll be my witness to his condition here this afternoon, of course."

"Of course."

The pair emerged from the commander's house into the bright day's glare. Already the bugle was resounding its blaring call on the quadrangle. "My squadron will be riding out within the hour," Frye declared. "I'll be saving time by not stopping at my own residence. My wife is likely to be, er, occupied. Pay my respects to her when you see her, Mr. Titus. You must excuse me now. I'm off to my office to pick up my saber."

"You're the first officer on the frontier that I've seen calling for his saber. I thought — "

"The saber is a noble weapon, sir! I keep my own polished, and not only for parades!"

He turned on his heel at the post commissary, and strode toward the stables and the paddock. Men were

164

pouring from the barracks and other buildings all around the compound. Frye was swallowed in the boot-stamping, rushing crowd of army men.

Hiram Titus watched, clenching and unclenching his pink, plump hands.

Marcus reined the big chestnut close to the towering canyon wall, nearly blinded by drifting gunsmoke and dust and glare. There was a skirmish of modest proportions going on. Comparatively few of Nantaje's warriors had been sent back to delay the troopers, while most of the Chiricahuas were probably taking positions for the main fray to come. Yet even a minor encounter with hostiles could be deadly. At least two Buffalo Soldiers who'd been blown from the saddle were sure casualties, as was Captain Jenks Wilcox.

He hadn't been able to keep tabs, in the confusion, on Wilcox and Sergeant Meadow, whom he'd last seen aiding the shot officer. Now the rataplan of gunfire turned sporadic, as the troopers massed behind boulder jumbles, through the ambush notch and down out of the narrows. Mescalero scouts had taken to the steep walls, scaling upward to get above the attackers, who were likely to be suicide fighters who would not give up till death.

An outbreak of shots halfway up the east slope signaled flare-up action. Marcus's eyes fixed on a steep transverse ledge forty feet from the floor. Two bronze figures reared in a hand-to-hand struggle, one an army scout, one a frenzied, determined Chiricahua. Nantaje's raider knocked the scout into a dense catclaw clump. The scout bounded back, with his knife flashing. The active forms locked for a few seconds, and then one hurtled, pinwheeling, into empty space.

The red headband of the victor proclaimed him a scout. The major left off holding his breath. All shooting ceased for several minutes. All up and down the crumbling, decomposed rock face Mescalero heads were popping up.

Desalin came up beside the chestnut on moccasined feet. "All Chiricahua *ha-tsals*, they are dead, Marcus Cavanaugh. Now these Buffalo Soldiers can move forward again on trail of Nantaje's big band of warriors."

"Might there be another ambush up the line?"

"Desalin, he think not this side of rancherias. Other side, down toward Mexico, there are many more good places for to trap Buffalo Soldier troops."

Marcus nodded thoughtfully. His gauntleted hand rested on his cantle pack. "Then we just push on? It's nearly nightfall already."

"Good to ride at night. Tonight is moon. Plenty good enough for seeing, getting through this not-so-rough place."

"You claim this stretch of ground we're covering isn't rough?"

"You wait, Marcus Cavanaugh. You will see the land on the other side. There the Thunderhorse's high walls have toppled. Many rock chimneys to be ridden around. Many deep barrancas. There are great shelves of red stone near the haunted mesa's base. Trails go among many-colored rocks. It has been said that only two creatures besides Chiricahuas may leave the strongholds and go south. They are the jackrabbits and the hawks."

"So, we'll be in for it?"

"That's so."

Marcus shouted. "Men, group up! Form your columns! Wounded to the rear for travois-trailing. First Sergeant Meadow! To me, if you please!"

The sergeant came trotting up. "Where's Captain Wilcox? What's his condition?" Marcus asked.

"Hit through the upper chest, Major." The horse and the bulky black man both shook heads. "Lost him a lot of blood, he did. He's back among those rocks there, on the ground."

"Take me to him."

Marcus saw as soon as he swung from the saddle that he'd be taking command. Wilcox lay slumped against a boulder, conscious, but with his face ashen beneath the sooty stubble on his chin. The great red stain across his front extended from collar to cartridge belt. "Did the slug pass on through?"

"Yes, suh," Meadow told him.

The captain smiled up at Marcus weakly.

"You don't need to tell me you're in pain, Wilcox. But we'll get you through this. Corporal Bogg, the trooper with medical training — he's being fetched. And Skibahete has his Apache herbs. Great infection-curbers. Help me get his blouse off, Sergeant."

It didn't look as though the wound needed to be fatal. At least the officer was far from dead yet. Wilcox's broad chest was pale under his blouse and underthings. Both entry and exit holes made by the bullet were puckered and blue.

"Don't worry about a thing, Captain. We won't abandon you, or the other casualties. Nor will we abandon this mission. Desalin says Nantaje's not far ahead. I aim to march the troops on through the night."

"I-I approve, sir," Jenks Wilcox croaked.

"Good man."

The men rested and tended the several wounded — and buried the one trooper who'd been shot dead. They didn't bother with killed hostiles. Marcus also ordered the evening meal; hardtack and canteen water. Of course, no fires. The scouts foraged scorpions and lizards to enhance their own meal. To them, food was food.

In the canyon depths, dusk was fleeting. The early moon washed the cliff walls with an eerie quicksilver sheen. The company was mounted and riding again, the horses weary and plodding ponderously. It was going to be a long and difficult night.

Nantaje's band filed into the moonlit glade surrounding the rancheria, their weary ponies shambling with their bagged and hide-wrapped hoofs. The wrappings had been intended to muffle tracks and make the party hard to follow, but the war leader had no doubt that the army's scouts — traitors to their own Apache blood — would follow, nonetheless. The pressure would be maintained. Nantaje wanted the wickiups of the People out of this place, their traditional stronghold. He wanted them transferred to the towering Sierra Range of Mexico.

The war leader hadn't liked the idea of the Buffalo Soldiers when they'd first appeared in these lands. He liked it even less now, with the persistent column breathing down his neck. They'd trailed him into his remote domain, unafraid of waiting perils. He'd watched their dust cloud in the desert as they'd pressed, and closed their distance. Still, all was far from lost. As things stood, Nantaje's Chiricahuas outnumbered the Buffalo Soldiers. And Nantaje's Chiricahuas were on their own home ground.

Still there was something that Nantaje felt, something about the Buffalo Soldiers' magic or the power they owned. The war leader was uneasy. The sooner he laid his ambush and killed them all, the better, his instinct told him.

In the center of the massed cluster of brush huts, the warriors threw themselves from their ponies' backs. Women, children, and old men emerged to greet the newcomers. A low babble of sound rose between the moon-sheened cliffs. There was laughter and excited talk.

Nantaje worked swiftly to hobble his pony and put it to graze. He glanced up to see Noohatacah standing over him. The venerable shaman's symbol-decorated shirt hung on his shrunken frame. He seemed to have lost a few more teeth. But the strong, dark eyes glittered like a snake's.

"So, Nantaje."

"Ho, my father."

"How go the White Eyes?"

Nantaje finished with his mount and stood up. "The bluecoats will come here, but they are not the White Eyes. They are the Buffalo Soldiers. Nantaje promises he will kill them all."

"Here?"

"South of here. On the land below the haunted hills." He explained quickly how the People would break camp this night, then lead the bluecoats to their deaths.

"You believe this plan will work, war leader?"

"Yes. My warriors are brave."

"It is well."

"I will tell everyone of my medicine," the shaman said. "How they must listen to your orders, Nantaje!"

" *Enju*, Noohatacah. There will be a dancing?"

"How soon must we break camp?"

"Very soon."

"There need be no dance. The People's warriors are strong. Kill the bluecoats under Thunderhorse, you say, Nantaje? The lightning god will help you."

Oddly, there was a flicker of faint lightning in the west. The moon fled behind a bank of scudding clouds.

"You've picked the place for your surprise attack?"

"The best place, *di-yi*."

"Your warriors will kill the Buffalo Soldiers."

" *Enju*."

Chapter Ninteen

Implacable heat on the vast desert griddle punished the Buffalo Soldiers of E Company. They had ridden up off the shadowy floor of the canyon when dawn was just a pewter smear. Now they passed through a graveyard of the titans, littered with immense stone monoliths. It had been an all-night forced march of the most grueling kind. Marcus's order had been to eat without stopping or leaving the saddle.

Some of the privates had seen the look on Marcus's face before the moon set, and found it incredibly harsh. The slanting planes had assumed an edge, and the eyes burned deep in their hollow sockets, set on the goal. Every man did his best to keep up, fearful of being left behind. Some were feeling the stupor of exhaustion. There was no trail that the ordinary troopers could make out, but the scouts knew what they were doing, and pushed on.

The stupendous rock formations finally blunted the senses. Gulches and coulees were threaded and crossed. There was no fresh water. Like men in a trance, they followed the lead of Marcus Cavanaugh, Sergeant Meadow, and the scouts. They passed along ledges where a single false step would have send mounts and riders plummeting. But no one's nerve cracked, and once more the column came through: officers, Buffalo Soldier riders, horses with litters for the wounded, and mules with packs.

They came to the deserted rancheria of Nantaje's people, and saw broken-down wickiups and abandoned skin-drying frames among the *jacals*, all evidence of a hasty departure. Marcus ordered them to press on.

Desalin trotted his mount up beside the major's. "They are only short hours ahead now, Marcus Cavanaugh. They have the women of the tribe and the children with them. They move slow."

Marcus cast a glance at the sky. Sweat had glued his shirt to his back and turned the inside of his campaign hat rancid. He held his face rigid as a stone. "Then we'll catch up with them today."

"Look ahead down there, Marcus Cavanaugh! Look!"

The column leaders had humped over a rock lip and confronted a ridge. It was dense with clumps of dry mesquite. Down this long descending rock spine, the route serpentined. The men had emerged from the claustrophobic walls, and could see quite far. They viewed a natural saucer, miles wide, and beyond that, the enormous massif that was Thunderhorse. The brooding mesa was cleft with fissures, its towering face hued amber and vermilion. Marcus's eye followed the Mescalero's pointing finger. In the great basin below, a tiny dust cloud plumed. Ant-sized specks crawled the surface of the land. Nantaje's party!

"How many fighting men would he have, Desalin?"

"Plenty more than this Buffalo Soldier bunch."

Marcus breathed. "Let me map some strategy. By the look of it, if they want to trap us, they must do so at the far end of the sink. There the route heads into another canyon maze, but after that there's open desert and no hope of surprise."

"They will wait for us at the place you say," the scout affirmed.

"The messenger-runner we sent back would've reached Bowie on the night before last. Colonel Thornhill was to send a squadron toward the border and intercept. If all's as expected, those companies are east of here by now. The trick will be to guide them to this point. Then the commanders can look down from this same vantage point. They'll see us out there, once we've advanced. I take it there's more than one way through the badlands?"

"Mescalero scouts can take troopers through."

"Good! Our companies can divide, and hit them from two sides!" Marcus gathered his reins, wheeled the chestnut around in place. "Sergeant Meadow!" The burly black wearing the cavalry-yellow chevrons trotted close. "I want a fire built on this high point," Marcus told him. "A huge fire. Put a detail to cutting brush. A lot of smoke will pull the squadron from Bowie here."

"Yes, suh!"

"Our main column will move on ahead, the fire-setters to catch up later. Now, move the march ahead, Sergeant!"

Labe Meadow did so.

From down in the basin, Nantaje saw the chimneying belch of smoke. "There," he exclaimed to his warrior friend Soojhamatahee. "Buffalo Soldiers, they are coming this way. Nantaje's warriors trap them all! Crows and buzzards will feast on their dead carcasses!"

Soojhamatahee was an exceptionally bloodthirsty man. "Ah, kill," he grunted gutturally to his chief. "Ah, kill!"

Sergeant Labe Meadow replaced his field glasses in their case and turned in his saddle. "I looked over our backtrail, Major Cavanaugh, suh, and the relief squadron's not in sight." The pair sat their mounts outside yet another canyon. This one opened at the mighty mesa's base, not particularly deep itself, but walled on one side by the vertical east face of Thunderhorse. The floor was rocky and choked with catclaw thickets. A wide trail of conspicuous tracks, those of Nantaje's party, led into it. It was clear that some of the Indians' ponies were weak and stumbling. It was shortly after midday. The sun, near its zenith, was brutal and hot. There was a long afternoon ahead, before the desert dusk fell.

"I want to engage the enemy today, Sergeant," Marcus said. "Their people are as tired as we are. We mustn't let them slip away. We'll put my plan in action by dividing our force, as I've explained. You know what to do with the twenty men you'll lead?"

"Yes, suh."

"The Apache scouts have moved out to deploy themselves?"

Meadow consulted his heavy stem-winder watch. "Twenty minutes back."

"Then, let's do this thing."

Marcus swung from the saddle, fisting his service revolver, and scanned the group of Buffalo cavalry as they stood afoot. All of them clutched loaded and readied Springfields. The big trap-door breechloaders were heavy weapons, but these men handled them as easily as toys. Marcus marked them as experienced, solid fighting men. The kind he could count on.

He glanced over his T-squared shoulder at the horse handlers and their charges. Everything appeared under control. There was no sense in uneasiness over the relief squadron's absence. They'd be arriving eventually. The thing he had to do now was pin Nantaje in, and he figured he knew just how.

Silently, he waved his men forward, and they began their slow advance. Afoot, they made lesser targets, and could get to cover quicker if they needed to. In this terrain, that was vital. In war, the unexpected took place too often.

They entered the canyon and hiked along the boulder-flanked trail. Nothing happened when they rounded the first bend, or the second. It was quiet in the shaded depths, the sky a blue ribbon high overhead. They heard and saw no birds. What had the scout Skibahete told him? Marcus remembered. That the absence of noise could spell trouble, as well as its presence.

The attack exploded around the soldiers in an echoing, deafening roar of shots. Great divots of earth erupted at their feet. Gunsmoke pillowed from the colorful looming rock walls.

The barrage came from halfway up the cliffs, and threw a deadly hail of lead. Marcus saw a trooper throw up his hands and go down. Dust spurts sprang from his form as yet more slugs impacted. There was no sense trying to save the man, for he was dead.

Marcus sprinted for the nearest shielding boulder, as did all the cavalrymen. One by one they were able to find shelter. They started returning a steady and accurate fire, and their 500-grain bullets tore into clumps of mountain shrubs that served as ambush points. Chiricahua warriors who'd been struck pitched out from behind their cover and lay still.

"Stay away from wounded broncos!" Marcus shouted. "They'll try and knife you, battling to the last!"

A slug spanged the stone face beside his ear, spattering chips. The major felt a jolt of pain as his ear was clipped. There was a trickle of warm blood. Marcus reared and fired his Colt. The young black man who'd holed up with him triggered his long gun. He let out a satisfied whoop. "I got me one, Major, suh!"

"Good man!"

"Firin' so fast, though, I be burnin' my poor hands!" He worked the trapdoor action to eject the cartridge, only to slide another round home. He aimed and triggered again. A yelp and a thud came from out on the flat. Marcus peeped with slitted eyes and saw a dead Apache.

The shielded troopers were in kneeling or prone positions, firing their carbines at the enemy doggedly, then reloading to keep up a hail. Out on the canyon floor, sun-yellowed smoke fogs drifted. Shots riddled the underbrush, sang in echo, each shot a seeming volley. Occasionally a bronco gave an exultant whoop. The Buffalo Soldiers held their ground and battled on.

Of course, there was no winning this kind of skirmish. Marcus had known it when he'd planned the advance. Now, here he was among the decoys, while the real strike force lurked and spied above. For if his dug-in force couldn't drive the redskins back, neither could they be dislodged by shooting snipers.

Like the tearing of an enormous canvas, the roar of new rifle fire tumbled through the pass. Clouds of powder smoke poured from the rocky maw ahead, while fleet Chiricahua broncos dashed along the canyon's floor. It was the big charge that the major had been waiting for.

Acting as bait to lure Nantaje to a decisive commitment, the cavalrymen had moved in. But half the Buffalo Soldier company had climbed the mesa by a hidden trail known to Desalin. The blacks had deployed themselves along the rimrock with the Mescalero scouts.

Now Marcus tore off his campaign hat and prepared to signal by hurling it in the air. In another minute the charging, exposed broncos in the canyon would be hit by a surprise volley. The marksmen on both rims would fire down bullets — plus a man-made avalanche of cannonball-sized stones.

Marcus waited. Finally he cocked his arm to direct his hat toss — and froze when he heard a piercing, startling sound!

A cavalry trumpeter was boisterously tooting the "Charge." Down the canyon and toward the hostiles galloped a roaring cavalry column. And at their head, slashing the air with saber sweeps, rode Captain Shelby Frye.

Chapter Twenty

The all-out horse charge presented a gallant show. The guidons that the leading troopers carried spanked and fluttered in the wind of passage. The surging legs of the mounts hammered. Carbines flashed in the sun. Captain Frye was in his glory, up on a dappled steed with a good strong stride.

But the horse was conspicuous and drew enemy fire, Marcus Cavanaugh saw from his shielded position. The whole charge was foolish — monumentally so. There'd been no strategizing by Frye with his senior officer in the field. And now the carefully laid trap of the up-top ambush was jeopardized.

Nantaje just might win this battle yet, and wipe out the bluecoats. After, wreaking death without mercy today, the renegade Apache would set all Arizona ablaze, slaughtering the settlers and holding up railroad construction. Cavanaugh cursed to himself. What was Shelby Frye, the desk soldier, doing heading up a charge against the fierce Indians? Marcus jammed his hat back on his head, and nudged his trooper companion.

"Time to move our asses out, man! Got your rifle there reloaded?"

"Yes, suh!"

"Then, let's go!"

In the tight confines between towering pillars, the horsemen were at a disadvantage. The cavalry's strength lay in its ability to cover distance fast. Here, there was little open ground, merely aisles between tumbled granite slabs. The Chiricahua broncos, fighting on foot, ran from shelter to shelter, firing around the boulders almost at will. The bluecoat riders were being mowed down. Screams of the wounded rent the dusty, smoke-choked air.

Still, Captain Frye refrained from having the "Recall" blown. Past running and plunging horses, Major Cavanaugh glimpsed the captain, mounted and spurring about in the melee, waving aloft his long curving blade.

A running bronco spotted Marcus for an officer and veered toward him. The Chiricahua brought up his cocked Winchester. Marcus shot him through the chest, and he dropped. A plunging cavalry mount rushed by, its saddle empty. The beast's flank and withers were drenched in crimson. Abruptly it was shot, too, and crashed down in kicking, screaming frenzy. As sometimes happened in battle, there was a lull in firing. Marcus seized the opportunity. "It's your major, men!" he shouted. "Listen to me! Get the hell off those horses! They make targets of you!"

A few riders within earshot caught the good advice. They jumped from their saddles to close with the enemy hand to hand. Now the Buffalo Soldiers were up and active. On all sides they blasted away with service Colts, blowing holes in broncos.

Marcus glanced around and saw a trooper's neck pierced by an arrow. To his left, he witnessed an Apache face punched by a slug. There was a sudden inward-sucking as the back of the dark head dissolved in shards.

"Major! Watch out!"

At the warning, Cavanaugh blinked and spun. A squat bronco launched a dive at the officer, his war club high and arcing downward. Marcus dodged at the last second, and the warrior plunged on past. Marcus shot him on the way by.

Up and down the canyon floor, chaos reigned. The rocks and passages were festooned with muzzle flame. A number of soldiers had bellied down and were firing upward. Some died in that position. A knot of soldiers had bunched to direct concerted fire. Lance-wielding Chiricahuas, mad with blood-lust, charged in. The soldiers scattered. Issue carbines boomed, and the red-skins' repeaters crackled and popped.

A downed Buffalo Soldier struggled up stubbornly, bleeding from his thigh. He fired his Springfield and a bronco pitched face forward, his nose a gaping hole. Other troopers helped wounded friends as they kept up steady firing. Corpses with glazed eyes lay sprawling. Against one boulder, dead soldiers' bodies heaped three deep.

But the troopers were finally getting the idea. Most were dishing out better than they were forced to take, and the canyon floor accumulated many warrior dead. And still the Springfields kept spitting lead. Four Apaches leaped from a boulder top. Troopers charged them, swinging rifles by their barrels. Hardwood stocks slammed the Indians' skulls. Two hostile warriors were clubbed to death. The rest turned tail.

As the battle sorted out, more Chiricahuas were forced toward the mesa's base.

"That's the way, men! Keep it up!" Marcus shouted.

Here and there amid the general fighting, officers and noncoms peered his way. Marcus spotted Lieutenant Quint, who waved, then shot a running warrior in the face. Sergeant Will Keogh snatched a fallen guidon and speared a bronco. Lieutenant Carl Durkey fought one-armed until a hatchet was buried in his brain. A Buffalo Soldier named Cable avenged the shavetail. Corporal Hannibal Bogg flapped his arms like a goose and collapsed. A whoop of triumph lifted. Marcus squinted through the smoke.

Nantaje!

The burly war leader ran afoot as did his warriors, dealing death with pistol and a hefty flint-headed axe. As Marcus watched, he accounted for two more casualties, then was lost behind a stampede of riderless mounts. Every chance he had, the major signaled to men and officers. The hostiles were to be forced under the mesa's looming bulk. It was a bloody job, but it was getting done. The army continued to carry the battle to them.

Now the Chiricahuas gave resistance in knots and bunches. Nantaje seemed to be massing warriors on the other side. The broncos were strung out beneath the opposite canyon wall, a hard-shooting line. Their defiant whoops told experienced troopers they were readying another massed charge. This would be their most furious, as they tried to finish the bluecoats.

He took great personal risk to do it, but Marcus Cavanaugh clawed his way to a crumbling boulder spire. With all his strength he hurled his hat up toward the sky. It kited against the rust-hued backdrop like a flying bird. Then from atop the tall mesa's face there came excited yells — and a roiling, drum-roll of thunder.

Cannonballs of stone plummeted down, shoved from the brink. The horrifying rain bounded off the cliff faces, hammering down relentlessly on those beneath, flinging men about like tenpins. Heads and torsos were mangled, smashed. Shrieks of broncos rolled forth in waves. Some Chiricahuas were crushed flat. Some died silently, some with shrill, throat-bursting screams. It seemed as.if tons of rock were raining from the sky. Flayed flesh and gore splashed across the canyon floor. The inclines ran with runnels of blood. Crushed bodies lay everywhere, legs and arms projecting grotesquely from piles of stone rubble.

But, not every Chiricahua was done for. From the canyon's far side, the soldiers saw movement through the swirling dust. A wailing chant rose from the depths of the cloud. These were warriors' death songs.

"Christ," Marcus Cavanaugh breathed from his rock perch. "The survivors will make a suicide charge!"

And they did.

There were but few of the renegade raiders left. These dashed madly in the direction of the cavalrymen, who opened up with reloaded guns. Apaches began dropping. Only one darting redskin dodged skillfully and got across. This was Nantaje. As Marcus watched tensely, the renegade closed with a powerfully built Buffalo Soldier. Marcus recognized the broad-shouldered, bull-necked black. He was Corporal Obie Hank, already owner of a prized Congressional Medal. The man had been a certified hero once before. Now he needed to repeat.

Hank was not particularly huge — no horse soldier was permitted to be. When the black man squared off with the Apache war leader, it was an even match for size. Nantaje carried his studded club, while Hank wielded the single-shot rifle that he'd just fired off.

Fierce eyes glittering with hate, Nantaje sprang in and launched a blow — and missed. Hank grimaced, and fetched the Springfield around. The sharp front sight dug a copper arm. Nantaje showed no pain. Rather, Nantaje countered with a high, vicious kick. A moccasined heel drove to Obie Hank's groin.

The black man vented a harsh grunt, and his face went gray. This time, Nantaje aimed his club at the buffalo-pelt head.

Marcus, from a distance of five feet, cocked his side-arm Colt, and drew a bead. Before the major could trigger, the trooper backpedaled, caromed off a boulder. He swung his rifle and the Indian's war club was struck to the ground. But Hank's own grip was loosed, and his firearm spun away. Instantly the big hands of the black wrapped around the redskin's neck.

Nantaje tried to twist aside, but in vain. The Buffalo Soldier squeezed, and his grip became bear-trap tight. Nantaje's eyes bulged, his painted face purpled. Then his tongue popped past writhing lips. His whole frame twitched. With a last tremendous wrench, Obie Hank lifted the Indian bodily.

There was a snap like the report from a whore's derringer when Nantaje's neck broke. Hank dropped the Indian and peered wildly around.

A sudden quiet reigned in the canyon's bowels, and that quiet was intense. There were no more living hostiles.

Marcus Cavanaugh muttered softly: "That does it for them, by God." Louder, he cried, "All right, men, let's see to our casualties! Get those wounded carried away from the dead. Has anybody seen Captain Frye?"

"Over here, Major!"

Marcus hurried in the direction of the call. A pale young private stood beside a sprawled form with officer's shoulder-boards. Shelby Frye had died instantly with an arrow protruding from his chest. His saber, still bloodless, was clutched in a death grip. The face between the flowing sideburns wore a strangely vexed expression. Dust had already filmed the empty eyes.

Marcus stood up and turned at a sound behind him. It was the scout, Desalin. "Ho, Marcus Cavanaugh," he said. "From top of the mesa we saw other Chiricahuas. Women and children of Nantaje's band. A few old men. They are riding fast on horses that will soon give out. They run toward Mexico."

"We can afford to let them go. We have our decisive victory. Where's Sergeant Meadow, Desalin?"

"Here," roared the Buffalo Soldier noncom. He was winded, having run down the mesa trail nonstop. "Suh," he reported. "I just came from Captain Wilcox. While we was a-whuppin' the renegades, the captain, he died of his wound."

"Jesus!" But Marcus's pause was only momentary. This day's victory was important, true, but it had been a very costly one. "I'll be ordering Lieutenant Quint to take over E Company when we head back to Bowie. Meanwhile, Meadow, detail a burial party. For our own dead, not Chiricahuas."

Marcus stood. The battle was over. Nintaje's threat to Arizona settlement was ended. And in the hot blue sky overhead, the buzzards had already winged into sight, their bellys waiting for the spoils of war.

When bloodthirsty Indians slaughter a wagon train, Major Marcus Cavanaugh leads an outpost of raw recruits and renegades into a full scale . . .

COMANCHE WAR

④